Seduced

Rita Award Winning Author

MOLLY
O'KEEFE

CHAPTER 1

May 15, 1867
One hundred miles southwest of Denver

MELODY HURST STARED unblinking at the cabin and wondered if she'd left her home in Georgia only to die here in this cold, foreign clearing.

"Go on now," said her husband, Jimmy, from the trees behind her.

"There's no one here." She pitched her voice low, though she didn't know why. There was no smoke from the chimney, no sounds from inside. The cabin, the almond-shaped clearing, the barn and the rocky outcropping it was built into—everything was still.

"Best be sure." She glanced at him, hiding in the brush to her right, and he lowered his rifle toward her and pointed at the door. His eyes cold and hot all together. "Go."

There was no choice, really.

She cast one fleeting, desperate look over her shoulder toward her sister, Annie, who was hiding with their horses in the trees near the barn at the other end of the hundred-yard field. Melody couldn't see her, and it was a blade to her heart to know she was out there.

I'm sorry I got you into this.

Marrying Jimmy after the war was supposed to give them security. Peace of mind. Protection. Because before the war, that was what the men she knew did. They cared for their women, their land, their horses. The war had changed everything, though, and if there were still men with the capacity for kindness, she did not know them anymore.

Her heart pounding in her throat, Melody stepped out from the tree line through the high grasses and flowers. It was a cloudy, gray afternoon, and the blooms in the clearing were closed up tight.

The simple log cabin was graced with an extensive covered porch complete with a railing and a chair—it was ludicrous, that porch on such a plain building. A bonnet on a donkey. But she imagined the owner of this cabin could sit, put his feet up, and look at the clearing, the flowers, the barn opposite and the snow-capped mountains in the western distance. His entire kingdom.

What a pleasure that must be for him.

A pleasure Jimmy and his Remington fully intended to rob him of.

Her whole life she'd been called too clever for her own good; she had manipulated more than her share of outcomes, but she could not conceive of anything that would get her and Annie out of this horror.

The porch was made from the trunks of saplings strapped together, and she nearly tripped walking across the uneven surface.

"Hello?" she called, her voice shaking.

Please don't be home. Please. Please don't be home.

They'd tracked Mr. Baywood across the West, missing him by a day in Denver. A fortuitous accident for Mr. Baywood, but Jimmy had been furious. Her arm still ached where he'd grabbed it in their hotel room, hard enough to leave purple-black smudges on her skin.

There was a chance that this might not be Mr. Baywood's claim. But having grown used to cruel fate and bad fortune in the years since The War of Northern Aggression started, she knew when those two evil specters were present. And they were here in this clearing.

She knocked on the door.

There was no answer.

Thank God.

Not that it would change anything for Steven Baywood. Jimmy meant to kill him. But at least she wouldn't be standing in the way when Jimmy gunned him down.

"He's not here," she said, in relief more than anything.

A sudden crack of rifle fire in the forest to the west scared a flock of birds from the trees and nearly sent her to her knees.

Jimmy ran from the forest and jumped onto the porch.

"He's hunting," he said, his entire body alight with malicious victory as he stepped past her to the door. He pulled the knotted string that released the bar inside to open the door and went into the cabin. "He's close. Get in here."

His glee set off a terrible anxiety in her chest. Panic roared through her and she was lightheaded with fear. Her hands went numb, her knees loose.

"You hear me, Melody?" he snapped, his joy at finding the man he'd been hunting replaced by irritation with her.

Usually she'd immediately placate him if they weren't setting an ambush. But the strict rules that she followed, in an effort to keep the violence against herself reduced to some manageable level, were wiped away by the specter of this larger violence.

"I'm going to check on Annie." She didn't wait for Jimmy's permission before lifting her faded blue skirts and sprinting across the clearing and into the forest.

Her sister—so calm, so familiar in their brother's old jacket, her glasses sliding down her nose—stood beside three horses who had long ago grown used to gunfire. They calmly nosed the pine needles on the ground, looking for grass.

We could ride away.

With Jimmy so preoccupied with Mr. Baywood, they could get on those horses and head west. Or back to Denver.

They had tried it once, with disastrous results. Jimmy had caught them outside of St. Joseph, hurt Melody so bad they'd had to stay for a week until she could move without pain. But certainly they'd learned something from that failure? How to cover their tracks better? How to move faster, ride all night?

The thought was mirrored in Annie's anxious and knowing brown eyes. She could practically hear her sister saying the words.

But Melody still remembered what Jimmy had said while beating her like a dog who'd disobeyed: *Next time it will be your sister I kick, and I won't stop.*

"We can't," Melody whispered, trying to talk both of them out of it. She'd done so little to protect her sister after the war, she had to try now. "We have no money. No means. He'd find us. Jimmy will kill Mr. Baywood, steal the gelding in the barn and find us within the day."

And kill you. He'd kill you, Annie.

Annie grabbed Melody's hands.

"I know."

"You go." Melody's fingers bit hard into Annie's, so hard her sister gasped. Or perhaps it was what Melody was suggesting that made her eyes go wide with horror and astonishment. "I'm serious, Annie. Get on the horse and go. I'll keep him here. He might—" Well, this was awful, but probably true nonetheless. "He might not care."

"I care and I will not leave you."

"Jimmy means to kill this man." A rare wave of hysteria swept over her. Mr. Baywood had been a Yankee soldier, a prisoner at Andersonville where Jimmy had been a guard during the last months of the war. Melody didn't know what happened between them, how Mr. Baywood had escaped or why Jimmy deserted and fled with him. All she knew was that somehow Mr. Baywood had betrayed him. And Jimmy had spent the last ten months tracking him down. "I don't know what his crimes are. I keep telling myself that perhaps he deserves it. That he might be an evil man. But he has...he has built a cabin. With the most ridiculous porch..."

Annie squeezed her hands until the pain snapped her back from the edge of panic.

"Perhaps it's not his cabin?" Annie asked.

The lunacy of false hope. Melody had clung to it too many times, only to feel it capsize under the weight of her grim reality. Melody closed her eyes, wishing all over again with every scrap of strength that she had left that she could somehow reverse every decision she'd ever made that led them to this clearing.

"Please go," she whispered. "You'll find work. You'll be safe."

"Not without you," Annie whispered. "This might not even be his cabin."

Melody took a deep breath and then another, reaching out again for the thin, unpredictable comfort of false hope, if for no other reason than to help her sister cling to hers. "Perhaps."

Hand in hand they turned and walked back to the cabin, going slowly to accommodate Annie's club foot, and because they were in no hurry to be party to an ambush.

"It's a fine porch," Annie whispered.

Melody bit back a sob.

INSIDE, JIMMY HAD made himself comfortable. He'd put the stack of newspapers he'd gathered traveling from town to town over the last ten months onto the table in the middle of the room. He'd taken one of the three chairs and set it to face the door.

His Remington was in his lap.

"Over there." Jimmy pointed to a low bench, with a homemade mattress, nestled into the shadows on the other side of the wide stone hearth, where dying embers barely glowed. Annie and Melody crossed the dirt floor, giving Jimmy, his Remington, and his unpredictable temper a wide berth, to sit down on the mattress. Hay crinkled beneath them, poking through the rough linen to jab Melody through her skirts.

Over the workbench on the far wall was a window covered with greased paper. On such a gray day it let in very little light. The shadows inside were deep and thick.

"How can you be sure this is Mr. Baywood's property?" Melody asked.

Jimmy pointed to the wall behind them. She and Annie both turned to see newspaper clippings tacked to the wall. News of a five-barrel petroleum distillery in Pennsylvania. The pages of a pamphlet called "Report on the Rock Oil, or Petroleum, from Venango Co., Pennsylvania."

"The daguerreotype," Jimmy said. "He had it in prison."

Next to an announcement proclaiming the Army's need for kerosene in the western forts was a faded daguerreotype of a family in their Sunday best. Three teenage boys and a younger girl, her hair still in braids, sat unsmiling at the feet of an older seated couple, whose clasped hands rested on the man's knee. The woman was trying not to smile.

Melody turned away, her eyes burning.

No more, she thought, her fingernails digging into her palms. *I can accept no more grief. I have enough of my own.*

An hour passed as if on the edge of a piano wire, and just when she thought she would scream from the tension and silence, there was a heavy thump on the porch, and a moment later the door swung open, letting in the cold bite of spring mountain air and a big blond man who, at the sight of Jimmy at his table, quickly lowered the rifle on his shoulder.

"Drop it," Jimmy said.

"You," Mr. Baywood said.

Melody sucked in a breath, and Mr. Baywood's eyes, blue as the sky, swung to her for a moment and widened in surprise.

"We start shooting in here, one of those women is likely to get hurt," Mr. Baywood said.

"Likely." Jimmy did not lower his gun, but after a moment Mr. Baywood did, setting it down on the dirt floor beside the door. And in that one chivalrous gesture, no doubt orchestrated his death.

He didn't seem to be scared, which was strange. Most people were scared of Jimmy, even if he wasn't lying in ambush and holding a gun on them. It was the deserter's brand on the side of his face, the ragged *D* over his cheek and across one eye.

"Shut the door. You're lettin' in the cold air."

Mr. Baywood shut the door, but not before Melody saw the dead turkey, plucked and dressed, on the porch. His hunt had been successful.

So had Jimmy's.

"How did you find me?" Mr. Baywood asked.

"You left a trail a letters."

Was it her imagination or did Mr. Baywood's shoulders slump?

"Those were for my family."

"Which I pretended to be. Since my homecoming in Georgia was not welcomin'." He turned his face slightly, and in the dim twilight the brand on his face was illuminated in macabre detail. "My wife and I went on to St. Louis, where I saw a notice in the newspaper that there was a letter at the post office for anyone with the last name Baywood. I got real curious. Could it be my partner—"

"We were never partners."

"You were singin' a different tune when I let you outta that hellhole. When I shared my rations with you." Jimmy's voice got low and flat, the sign of his temper rising.

"I did not force you to desert. You agreed to my plan and came on your own, and it's not my fault you were stupid enough to be caught by the home guard."

"You left me for dead. Ran away the second you heard trouble."

"I can't imagine you wouldn't have done the same. There is no love lost between us, Jimmy. I gave you the means with which to escape the Confederate army. A Reb solider returning an escaped Yankee prisoner of war was a lie that most would have believed."

Melody had learned that averting her eyes, or even closing them, did not stop anything. It made no horror disappear, no atrocity—it only made the shock of opening her eyes worse. She'd hid her head under a pillow for the first part of the war, only to emerge blinking and useless to a changed world.

She would not do that again. So she held her eyes open with such force they started to water.

Don't look away. Don't. Your husband will kill that man, and closing your eyes will not make that go away.

Bearing witness to it would not change it, but she was compelled nonetheless.

"This is real nice land you got here," Jimmy said, so casual. "Read about your claim in the papers. Right next to an article about there being rock oil in these parts."

"What is your point?" Mr. Baywood asked through gritted teeth.

The explosion lifted Mr. Baywood off his feet and threw him against the wall. His hat rolled to the door.

The sound of Jimmy shooting Mr. Baywood boomed inside the sturdy timber walls. Chinking rattled down from between the logs to the dirt floor, and blood flooded into Melody's mouth where she'd bitten her tongue. There was a scuffle she couldn't see because of the shadows and the smoke, followed by a hard crack and a fleshy thud. Jimmy walked to the door and opened it, clearing the smoke and letting in enough light that she could see Mr. Baywood on the ground, blood oozing from a wound in his stomach. Jimmy grabbed him by the foot and dragged him out to the porch.

Gut shot. *Oh. Oh, Lord.*

Annie's lips began to move in prayer.

Jimmy stepped back into the room and Melody lifted her head, met his eyes.

"Don't touch him," he said. "He's gonna die real slow."

He grabbed his hat from the table and walked back out the door.

Melody and Annie shared a shocked look before Melody jumped to her feet. She swallowed back her bile and stepped over the shot man and the dead turkey, running after Jimmy through the forest to where they'd hidden the horses.

"Where... where are you going?"

"To find an oil prospector," he said, untying Melody's brother's horse, Jacks. Jacks didn't like Jimmy and he shook his head, shying away as Jimmy tried to mount him. "Figure out how this oil business works."

"Where?"

"Pueblo or Denver."

She swallowed her gasp. It had taken three days across the high plains to get to these foothills. Three days.

"How long will you be gone?"

"A week or more, I imagine."

He was leaving her and Annie for a week, alone in this cabin, miles from anything. She was torn apart by relief and fear. A week without him. With just Annie, a gut-shot man and whatever lived in these woods.

"That man... What..." She glanced at the cabin as if it might have answers. "What do I do?"

"Leave him."

"What about wolves? Indians?"

Jimmy looked around at the pine trees that surrounded the clearing and finally pulled his carbine rifle from the scabbard across his horse's flank. "Don't let them burn the cabin or take you."

He handed her the gun, wheeled Jacks around and was gone, through the shadows in the trees, back toward the well-worn trail to Denver.

His leaving was shocking, but not all that surprising. Jimmy didn't sit still. Not since the war. She'd thought when they were married, and he'd moved into her home, that he would replant the fields. Repair the outbuildings. That he would try, as he'd promised, to rebuild her family's property. But he could not even sit at a table without being blind drunk. He roamed the house at all hours, drinking and cursing, waking her up to yell at her, about crimes he suspected her of plotting against him.

Most nights he passed out on the porch. A gun in his hand.

Within a month he'd sold her home to some Northern carpetbagger who didn't know the first thing about cotton or horses. And soon they were moving across the West without rest. Without a plan, that she could tell.

And then Jimmy found that letter in St. Louis, and he'd become a bloodhound after Mr. Baywood.

After an incredulous moment and a prayer for strength, Melody picked up her skirts to run back to the house.

Annie was already bent over the man on the porch, her sleeves rolled up, her fingers searching through the hole in the man's stomach. A red knot had risen up on his temple.

Mr. Baywood was passed out, whether from pain, blood loss, or the wound to his head it was hard to know. But his chest was still moving, so he wasn't dead yet.

"I can't believe it, but he missed everything important. Leastways that's how it feels."

"He's not gut-shot?"

"No. Went clean through his side. Go back to the horses and get my saddlebag."

"You think you can save him?"

"Maybe. Go get Father's bag."

Melody nodded, but for a moment her feet didn't obey.

"Melody—"

"If we save him, where do we hide him? Jimmy will be back in a week."

Annie glanced up. "I'll say it was me. That you didn't help."

"He'll kill you."

"Maybe."

"I won't let you die because I'm scared of a beating."

But it wasn't just a beating. They both knew it. And though she'd managed to avoid his bed all but three times since her wedding night a year ago—not a terribly difficult feat due to his increasing need for whiskey in order to sleep at night—the specter of it was enough to keep her living in fear. And she was ashamed of her fear. She was. But that didn't change its presence.

"Chances are I won't be able to save him anyway," Annie said. "But this way, we won't have wolves or worse all over us in the morning, because we left a dying man on the porch. Go. Get my things."

Melody ran back to the horses and unfettered them, leading them from the copse of pines closer to the house where they could graze. She'd put them in the barn later. Snow was starting to fall. Back home, in May the last of the azaleas would be in bloom, and Mama would start napping on the porch—

Don't. Don't think about it.

It took her three attempts to tie the horses to the porch, her hands were shaking so hard. Once it was done, she hoisted the saddlebags up onto her shoulder and stepped back over the turkey and Mr. Baywood to get back inside, not looking at either of them.

Annie had thrown Jimmy's newspapers into the hearth and built a crackling fire.

"I need help dragging him in," she said and Melody nodded. "We'll never get him off the ground, but I won't try to take out that bullet outside away from the fire."

Melody grabbed the man's slack hands, Annie took his legs, and using all their strength, they dragged the man back inside through the puddle of his blood. He didn't twitch or move.

"Why isn't he waking up?"

"Jimmy must have kicked him or hit him with his pistol. Here." Annie touched the pronounced bump that was turning purple on Mr. Baywood's head. "Can you find some whiskey?"

Melody searched while Annie took off the man's shirt and pulled their father's medical kit from the saddlebags.

"You've done this before?" Melody asked, looking on the shelf over the workbench. She found a nearly full bottle behind a bag of sugar.

"Many times."

Annie, who had no hope for a match due to her leg, the stammer she'd had when she was younger and what Mama used to call an odd nature, had followed their father into field hospitals during the war.

Before he died, Father had called Annie, with great pride, the best assistant he'd ever had.

Melody had spent that time embroidering the initials of her fiancé, Christopher, on handkerchiefs and blissfully planning a grand wedding that would never happen. Mama used to say that one of her daughters had to be a changeling. It was the only way to explain having girls who were so vastly different.

Annie took a pair of forceps from the old leather bag, poured whiskey over them and then took a big swig herself.

"Annie!" Melody cried, having never seen her sister drink spirits at all, much less right from the bottle. Mama would have fainted at the sight.

All of this—every bit of what they were doing—would have sent Mama to bed with her Bible and despair.

Annie handed the bottle to Melody. "The light in here is too poor for my eyes. I will need you to close the wound, so perhaps something to steady your hands would be a good idea."

In the candlelight, the body between them, Melody had never seen Annie so in command of herself. Of her setting.

Her countenance, her solid and steady demeanor proclaimed that it would be okay.

This was Annie at her best, and Melody took sudden and strange comfort in it. And the ridiculousness of this situation faded away and became one more element of their survival.

Surgery was a thing they had to do to get to the next thing.

Melody needed very little encouraging, and she took her own burning gulp of the whiskey.

Finally, at Annie's nod, she crept around to the bleeding man's head and leaned her weight on his shoulders in case he woke up and took exception to Annie digging in his side.

But he didn't even twitch and Annie made quick work of getting the bullet.

"If he was trying to kill Mr. Baywood, your husband is a terrible shot," Annie said, holding the bullet up to the firelight.

"It's the brand. He's nearly blind in his right eye."

"But he was standing about five feet from him."

"Are we grateful he's a bad shot or not?"

Annie smiled and then did her best to flush out the wound with the water from the bucket they'd found by the fireplace, until the both of them were kneeling beside Mr. Baywood, in a lake of bloody, muddy water, their skirts sodden. Annie moved out of the way, and Melody stepped in with the surgical needle and silk thread from Father's bag.

But faced with a bloody gaping hole in a man's side, she suddenly doubted the strength of her embroidery skills.

"How do I...?"

"Pretend he's silk on a hoop."

"My imagination isn't that strong."

"You just do it," Annie said, level and brave. "We have done worse."

If she can take out a bullet, I can stitch him up.

Melody took another swig of whiskey and pressed Father's heavy surgical needle through Mr. Baywood's flesh. It did not give easily, and she had to *push* the steel through the skin. It pulled and tugged as she shoved it through the flesh.

Bile filled her throat, but she fought it down again and again until she was done.

"You did it!" Annie said, her pride a lovely thing.

"I suppose I did," she said, grateful that something from her empty and useless life before the war had been repurposed into something of value.

CHAPTER 2

JUST AFTER DAWN, Melody woke Annie from the bed in the corner where she'd collapsed not too many hours ago.

"I need to find water," she whispered. "A fever set in."

"How is the swelling around his eye?" Annie woke up quickly, her mind immediately back to worry.

"Worse. It's spreading across his forehead."

"Do I need to bleed him?"

She could not even begin to answer that question, no matter how badly her sister needed the reassurance of a knowledgeable opinion.

"Annie, I am no doctor's assistant. I'm sorry. That decision is yours and I'm sure whatever you decide is the right answer. I'm to fetch water."

Annie fumbled for her spectacles and pushed herself off the bed. Her brown hair was a wild mess of dandelion fluff, and Melody smiled and patted it down like she would have years ago.

It was a luxury to touch someone with kindness, instead of in fear or desperation. She'd forgotten what that felt like. How it breathed air into her dark and fearful spirit.

Annie grabbed her hand, her eyes a hard brown beneath

the glass. "We'll be fine. As long as we're together."

"Yes, we will."

They said it to each other every morning. A pact started that first morning after her wedding, when Annie had found her so bloody and battered on the floor beside the bed in their parents' old bedroom.

Melody gently curled her fingers with her sister's.

Calm, she thought. *Soft. We need not grab onto each other for life right now.* With one last ineffective pat to her sister's hair, Melody took the bucket and stepped outside, hoping to find a well or stream in the clearing.

The turkey was still on the porch. She sniffed it but didn't smell any rot. The cold overnight had worked in their favor.

The clearing was a sea of white, blue, purple and pink blooms, their petals open to the bright sunlight. Lupines and columbine, she'd heard them called.

If she'd had any wonder left in her, it would have been stirred by such a sight.

But no matter how beautiful the setting, no one built a cabin far from water.

There was no other well-worn path into the woods, besides the one that led toward Denver. No sound of a stream either.

She crossed the clearing to the barn. Last night, after Mr. Baywood had been stitched up, she'd taken their horses, Lilly and Rue, inside and removed their saddles. It was tight in the barn, which now held three horses, a goat, two chickens and a bossy rooster. But it was warm and cozy. When she entered, Lilly and Rue lifted their noses in welcome.

Mr. Baywood's gray horse was in the far stall, its back to the room. Put out, perhaps, by the sudden company.

It was one of those sturdy mountain horses they'd seen more and more often since crossing into Colorado. On the ground in front of it she noticed a pail half full of water.

There must be water close, she thought. The goat stood in the far corner of the barn, where the air was the coolest. But there was something odd about that wall, and as she walked closer she realized the stone wall wasn't whole, it was actually two walls. One in front of the other. Between the two there was a crack, nearly impossible to see in a passing glance.

Breathless with surprise and hope, she stepped into the fissure, and after a few feet, the crack widened into a chamber. With a spring, bubbling in its center.

She tasted the water, and it was ice cold and clear and sweet.

Relief made her sag against the cold, hard earth.

The ground surrounding the spring was wide enough for Mr. Baywood's body if they could drag him this far without killing him. They could hide him here until he got better or died and hope that Jimmy never found him.

"For these small things we are grateful," she murmured, but wasn't entirely sure she meant it.

She didn't have Annie's kind soul. What little kindness she'd been born with had been beaten right out of her, and she cared only about survival. Hers and her sister's. At some point she had to believe this nightmare would end. That they would find some amount of peace.

Annie still wanted to do what was right, what they'd been taught as girls a lifetime ago, but Melody saw little point in that if it got them killed.

And should Jimmy find this man alive, he'd kill them all.

THE TURKEY WAS off the porch, and inside Annie was mixing laudanum for Mr. Baywood. The soaking-wet dresses they'd worn yesterday were hanging over the chairs, steaming beside the crackling fire.

Annie had raked the ground, trying to spread the mud they'd made more evenly so it might dry faster in the sunlight that streamed through the open door.

"He's unconscious," Melody said. "What does he need the laudanum for?"

"I thought maybe we'd put him on Lilly, ride out until we

found a cave or someplace to hide him. I want to have some ready in case he wakes up."

"There's a cave with a spring in the barn," she said. "We can hide him there."

Annie put the cork back in the laudanum.

The turkey was spread out on the table. "What are you doing with it?" Melody asked.

Annie pointed to a large pot. "Smoke some, make stew with the rest. This house is bigger than you'd think. There's another room behind the fireplace."

Melody ducked through the small doorway to see into the hidden room. At the moment it was full of burlap bags of potatoes and flour, but she imagined he built it with family in mind.

"Jimmy said Mr. Baywood was expecting his family," Melody said, setting down the bucket. The log cabin was small but well made, almost no drafts coming through the timber of the walls. The chinking looked new. The stone fireplace was large with a wide hearth. The table and chairs were sturdy, made from the pine trees surrounding the place. There was food hanging from burlap bags and the air smelled of mud and fire and whatever plants were hung by strings from the rafters to dry.

If Mr. Baywood didn't survive, his murderer would make this her home. The thought made her nauseous and she pressed a hand to her belly. She'd done some truly reprehensible things in her life and paid for them in blood and grief. But taking the home of a man her husband had killed...

What did I do to deserve this? She wondered. *Or worse, what will be asked of me to pay for it?*

Before the war she'd craved attention and status. Reveled in her position of prestige, enjoyed the envy of other girls and the attention of all the men. She'd been selfish and conniving to serve her own goals. But for all of that, she'd had a dream that kept her alive through the war—of a family, of a husband

and children, of work that would bind them together. A fine legacy built and cared for with her own two hands. A home.

She had schemed to win Christopher, a man she'd thought would best make real that dream. Mama had told her that Christopher was too weak to match her, that he would wander or feel bullied, and part of her knew that Mama was right. But she'd thought she could control him. And that it would make her happy.

And she believed, with all that was left of her heart, that the cost of her hubris had been the destruction of her dreams. The war had taught her that every moment of happiness, no matter how slight, how meager and threadbare, would be paid for with an equal measure of sorrow. With despair.

And that the surest way to bring destruction upon the things she wanted was to want them in the first place.

Her dreams had not survived her dreaming them; they'd been broken and repaired, only to be smashed again and again. Each aspect compromised over and over. She'd wanted fine gowns, and instead had threadbare rags. She'd won Christopher, only to have him die in the first year of the war, and instead she got Jimmy, his younger, lesser brother, one of the few boys to come home at all.

Despite Annie and Melody's efforts, without the slaves the cotton fields went to seed, and then the hay pastures, until all that was left were the kitchen garden and the fruit trees, which she was barely able to keep alive, while Annie tried to hunt whatever game still lived in the forests around their land.

Most of the animals were taken by soldiers on both sides, until she and Annie learned how to hide them better when the armies marched past. Jacks, Lilly, and Rue were the only horses left from Father's fine stable.

The home she craved sold off to a man who would not ever love it as she had. Not ever.

Before the war, when she'd been vying for Christopher's attention, she'd wanted romance. Passion. Stolen kisses.

Rushed, panting caresses.

But all of that had been beaten and raped out of her.

Her dream was utterly unrecognizable to her now. She looked at those broken pieces and didn't know what she wanted.

To eat until she was full? To have enough food so her sister's stomach didn't growl at night?

To wake up in the morning without fear?

She'd married the wrong man for all of that.

But worse, perhaps she was the wrong woman for all of that. A soul not meant for dreaming and unable to hold onto happiness.

"How do we get him to the barn?" Annie asked, pulling Melody from her grim thoughts.

"We could put him on the blanket," Melody said, grateful that there was always work to keep them moving. "Remember how we got that dead Yankee out of the stream at home?"

Annie nodded, but looked down at her foot as if doubting its ability to do the work. It was odd to see her sister so hesitant. Ever since the war had required them to shed their ball gowns and get their hands dirty, Annie had thrived. The shy wallflower with a stammer had been trampled by a woman who seemed unaware of her limits.

"Are you well?" Melody asked.

"The ride has made me sore."

"Why didn't you say so?"

Annie laughed. "We've had our hands full."

"We can do this."

"There isn't any other choice, is there?"

"No."

They rolled Mr. Baywood onto a blanket and then began the torturous effort of

dragging him to the cave. His wound opened. Annie fell, her bent leg twisting underneath her. Melody felt muscles along her back straining and pulling.

"A little bit further," she groaned, helping her sister to her feet.

Inside the barn, Annie wiped sweaty hair off her forehead and cried with utterly out-of-place delight, "Chickens!"

Out of breath, Melody smiled and sagged against the wall.

At the spring they checked his wound, which was seeping but not bleeding too heavily, and wrapped him with blankets to keep away the chill. Faint sunlight would come in through the entrance if they kept the barn door open; otherwise the room was dark as a tomb.

"He's probably still going to die," Annie whispered, saying aloud what she probably didn't want to think.

"But we've done our best," Melody said, stroking her sister's back. "Father would be proud."

"Mama would be mortified."

"And my husband will be murderous." The words spilled from her lips without thought.

Melody felt her sister's eyes upon her cheek.

"If I could take the pain—" her sister whispered.

Melody squeezed her sister's hand because there was no point in regrets. Her sister had done a kind and noble thing; Melody would pay the bloody price of it. "Come, there's still much work to be done."

ON THE NINTH day of Jimmy's absence Melody milked the goat and Annie boiled the milk with some of the precious vinegar they had left, and they ate the delicious curds with their fingers, sitting on the porch, watching the bobbing flowers in the cool, sweet breeze.

But Melody was blind to it, her body sick with dread.

"Perhaps Jacks threw Jimmy off the mountain?" Annie asked, but Melody could not joke. Her stomach was acid and bile. Her head hurt, her body felt heavier than she could carry. Every minute of every day that passed she thought of Jimmy. Every rustle in the forest sounded like his return and the end of her reprieve. The endless work required of them barely distracted her, but as the days wore on she wanted him to return just to end the agony of waiting. She felt like a prisoner awaiting her trip to the noose.

"I cannot allow myself to pretend he won't be back," she whispered. She could not enjoy these days without him, free from the threat of violence or the soul-crushing work of managing his temper.

Look at what he has made me, she thought, near tears.

Annie gave her the last curd.

The next morning Melody woke up alone in the cabin.

Today, she thought, half prayer, half curse, *today he will come.*

She pulled on a shawl and slipped her feet into her boots before grabbing the last of their dried fruit and a piece of turkey breast to take out to her sister.

When Melody walked into the cave, Annie was digging through Father's medical

bag. Mr. Baywood lay silent, still unconscious though no longer feverish, beside her.

"Did you sleep out here again?" she asked Annie.

"No. I came out a while ago." The two of them were working in shifts, only able to leave him alone for an hour before one of them felt compelled to check on him.

"Has he eaten anything?"

"Broth. Some water."

Melody sighed and sat next to her sister. Mr. Baywood was getting pale and thin. Which made the yellow, purple and green bruising on his temple and face even more striking.

"Perhaps I should have bled him," Annie said. "Perhaps the pressure there on his temple is what keeps him asleep."

Annie had been rolling this decision over for days, first one way and then the other, constantly blaming herself for Mr. Baywood's not fully waking up.

"Last night," Melody said, leaning into her sister's side. "When I was out here, he told me that I was a good soldier.

That my mother would be proud."

She thought of Mama, whose pride in her dead son did nothing to assuage her grief. But as useless as they might be, she hoped her brother had heard similar platitudes from other soldiers as he lay dying.

"I don't know what to do for him." Annie's thin shoulders were bent under her defeat. "I keep looking in this bag like I'll find something."

Melody pressed the turkey and fruit into her sister's hand and said what she'd been thinking for days. "It would be better if he died."

"Melody—"

"Jimmy will be back. We can't hide him forever."

Annie gave her one of her disgusted looks, took the turkey and left.

Later that day, Melody came out of the barn with eggs only to find Annie digging up the clearing, through all the white and purple blooms.

"What are you doing?" Melody asked, as Annie drove sticks into the ground.

"I'm counting," she answered, using her lurching step to measure off another parcel of land. When she stopped she drove another stick in the ground, twisting it into the soil until it stayed upright. "Planning the garden."

"Why?"

"Mr. Baywood is dying."

Annie pushed her hair from her forehead and Melody saw the tears on her cheeks. The sight ran through her like a knife and she wished the right decisions could just stay right. That for once pain was not their constant companion.

"This isn't our land."

"Jimmy means to make it so."

The sun fell down between them in great golden sheets, from a sky so blue it seared the eyes. Truly Melody had never seen such light, such a pureness of air. She wished she could suck it all in, and through some alchemy apply it to her own black heart.

"I want to tend the living, instead of the dying. What is the harm in that, in planning for something that will grow? That we can tend and it will survive? I want to care for something and be nourished by it in return. That is what I want." Annie wiped the tears from her face and crossed her arms over her thin cambric shirt. She wore it tucked into her durable brown skirt and looked like a defiant farmer's wife.

Melody wore an old silk ball gown. The seed pearls had been sold off. The ribbons and lace were long gone. Now it was just a tawdry red silk that did not keep out the cold.

She'd been married in this dress, and the thought was so black, she fought it. Pushed it away as best she could. With as much force as she could muster she shoved all the black thoughts away and conceded once more to her sister's better self.

In the ten months of hard travel, the year of her marriage and the war before that, in the times when she would give in to despair or anger, her sister always managed to find some branch of hope to cling to.

A garden. Why the hell not?

"Let's plant," she said.

It took the better part of the afternoon, but when it was done they had turned over the loamy black soil and gotten rid of the rocks. They'd created a plot, far smaller than the one they'd had at home, but still respectable.

Melody was dirty and worn out, but pleased in a way she hadn't been since after Fort Sumter when she'd watched Christopher in his dress uniform, her lips still buzzing from his kiss, march off to what she'd been so convinced was sure, heroic victory.

Melody lifted the metal cup of cold water they were sharing in a toast. "To growing something," she said.

That's when Jimmy showed up.

CHAPTER 3

"I'M BACK, WIFE," he hollered.

Relief and horror were an awful combination, and she felt it all through her body. Under every inch of her skin. With a year's worth of practice to draw on, Melody stilled her reaction, the shudder of fear. Of revulsion. And after one shaking breath she managed to turn to her husband, with the best smile she was capable of. Only to stumble when she saw the stranger in black ride up behind him.

"Oh," Annie whispered. "Heaven help us."

The stranger was tall and lean, his face whiskered. Another time, in another place, his black eyes might have been considered handsome. But now, in this field surrounded by an air of violence and danger that was so palpable, so real as to be nearly visible, all she could think was, *This is the devil come to visit.*

"Melody," Jimmy snapped and she tore her eyes from the stranger and smiled at her husband, wearing her charm and manners like a dress that no longer fit, because Jimmy demanded it. Not in so many words, of course. She doubted he had the intelligence to understand that. But it was a part of what she'd learned managing his anger.

And she welcomed the part, the distance it gave her

between the woman married to that monster and what was left of the woman she'd been. The woman who'd turned the soil behind her. It was strange to realize now that she relished her performance, because it no longer bore any resemblance to who she was.

"Welcome back," she said, crossing the small patch of grass toward the horses. Jacks, she noticed, looked hard used, and she wished she could kick her husband with the same spurs he'd used against Jacks's white hindquarters. "You had a successful trip?"

"I found a prospector," Jimmy said, cutting a glance to the stranger, who stared at her with hard eyes. Sweat broke out under her arms. But she lifted her ratty, dirty skirt in the curtsy Mama had taught her, as if he were a gentleman come to call.

"A pleasure to meet you…"

"Cole, Mrs. Hurst," the man said, tugging on the brim of his hat. "Cole Smith." The name was dubious. They had traveled with a lot of Smiths after the war, men leaving past deeds behind. It did nothing to instill confidence in this man who seemed more sword than flesh.

"Welcome, sir. Please, call me Melody—"

"Call her Mrs. Hurst," Jimmy said, his smile a slice in his marred face. "I like that."

Cole Smith continued to stare at her, as if gauging her reaction, so she gave him none. "Allow me to introduce my sister, Annie Denoe," she said, pointing toward Annie, where she clung to the shadows of the porch.

"Ma'am," he said again with that dip of his head.

"She don't talk," Jimmy said, unbuckling his saddlebags and letting them fall to the ground before dismounting. "A mute gimp."

Melody felt her skin glow red hot but she kept her eyes on Jacks, reaching for his reins as Jimmy picked up the bags and headed for the barn.

"The women will take your horse," Jimmy said over his

shoulder.

The stranger shook his head. "I care for my own."

Melody gave the stranger her most dazzling smile, the one that had helped her snare Christopher before the war.

To think that had once been my finest accomplishment.

"It's quite all right," she said. The stranger could not go into the barn, not with Mr. Baywood there. Her head spun at the thought. This man did not seem as if his hands were clean in the moral sense, but Jimmy would kill him just for being here if he found Mr. Baywood. Jimmy was a man who covered his tracks in a very brutal way. "We have room to spare."

"You're well outfitted." His eyes seared over her skin, and she was sure he could see the lies and sweat on her. His words sounded like an accusation and she pretended her feathers were ruffled by his insinuations.

"My husband has taken great care in securing us this home."

Not quite a lie, but she felt the false bottom of it and knew if pressed it would collapse. She would collapse.

His black eyes narrowed, but he said nothing.

"I'll camp." He pointed to the copse of trees on the far side of the clearing, away from the barn but facing the front door to the house. "My horse will stay with me. But water would be appreciated."

"Of course," Melody said with a smile. "I'm assuming you will be joining us for dinner."

"Only if there's enough."

That made her pause. The world was hungry since the war, no one turned down a meal.

"Judging by my husband's saddlebags he has bought provisions. Why, it will almost seem a party, won't it?"

After nodding politely, Cole clucked his horse into motion, walking away from Melody. Annie rushed to her side. As Cole walked past the porch, he stopped, something on the wood gathering his attention.

The bloodstain.

They'd scrubbed it best they could, but the heart of the red stain remained, screaming violence. After a long, agonizing moment Cole moved on.

Melody let out a breath and rested her head against Jacks's neck. Her hands shook, her legs felt like water. "What have we done?" she whispered.

But Annie did not answer. Annie did not talk when Jimmy was near. It was as if she'd reverted back to the girl she'd been before the war. Shy and silent. But watching. Always watching. It was a trick she'd refined in ballrooms, much to Mama's dismay.

There were times Melody wanted to shake her. Force her to talk, because she could not stand the silence. Could not tolerate for one more moment just the sound of Jimmy's voice in her ear.

But in many ways it was Annie's way of protecting herself, by not attracting Jimmy's notice.

The way Melody wore her charm and grace, Annie wore her silence.

And both acts made Melody feel alone sometimes. Alone inside a cage.

This is no time to fall apart.

"We just need to keep them away from the spring," Melody said and Annie nodded. Together they walked toward the barn, leading Jacks. But Melody felt the burn of the stranger's eyes on her back as she walked. There was no telling what he thought of her, but as long as it wasn't the truth, they were safe.

"I'll stay here," Annie said.

Melody nodded, thinking of her husband making a meal of Annie and her leg and the way she allowed him to think she was mute. Annie was not bothered by the names Jimmy called her, the abuse he heaped on her head, but there were times Melody could barely stop herself from leaping to her feet and scratching out his hateful eyes. His malicious tongue.

"Keep Mr. Baywood quiet."

"You?" Annie whispered.

Melody squeezed Annie's hand. "I will be all right."

Another lie with a false bottom.

MRS. HURST WAS a china doll. A beautiful, fragile doll. If Cole were to grab her wrist, he was sure she would shatter.

Mrs. Hurst was also a very unwelcome and unexpected complication.

He'd been in Denver three days when he heard the news that there was a blond man with a deserter's brand staying over at Delilah's looking for a rock oil prospector. And Cole had been following a blond man with a deserter's brand for months.

Cole had gone to Delilah's and there Jimmy sat, slouched over the bar. He had kept his hat pulled low, but in the bright sunlight coming through the door he could not hide that *D* scarring his flesh, high on the cheek, nearly obliterating one eye.

There simply was not enough coincidence in the world, so Cole put his hand out and said, "I hear you're looking for a prospector."

After an interview that consisted mostly of Cole buying Jimmy something to drink and saying all the words he knew as they related to oil prospecting, he was hired. He'd learned early on as a bounty hunter that lies were mostly about confidence and eye contact. Cole named a price, Jimmy agreed and paid half up front, and then Cole followed him from Denver up to this clearing. To this cabin with its bloodstained porch.

And two women.

Melody slid a dried venison steak that she'd boiled onto his tin plate and followed that up with a scoop of beans, carefully attempting to hide the bruises on her arm with the small sleeve of her gown.

"Thank you, ma'am," he said and she nodded, her smile brief and practiced before being quickly put away.

Thirty seconds in that clearing and he'd known three things.

The horses were hers.

Jimmy hated his beautiful wife as much as he wanted to own her.

And, most importantly . . . this land wasn't his.

But Cole couldn't be sure that it was his brother's. Yet.

Initially, Cole had thought he was tracking his younger brother Gavin, but the rumors said that the man gathering Steven's letters from the newspapers had a Georgia home guard brand on his face. Gavin was from West Virginia and Cole could not imagine his baby brother deserting anything.

So he'd given up on the stranger being Gavin, but continued to track the man who was pretending to be kin, picking up the letters Steven had left behind.

But in all those months of following Jimmy, talking to innkeepers and bartenders and the newspaper men with their black fingers, there'd never been mention of a wife. Or a mute, gimp sister.

Had Jimmy hid them so well? Or was this the wrong man?

For taking his brother's letters, Cole meant to question Jimmy. For killing Steven and squatting on his land, should that be the case, Cole would kill the coward.

But what the hell was he supposed to do with Jimmy's wife?

He'd killed a woman, once. Tracking a man and his partner who'd robbed a wagon train and shot a sheriff. He'd tracked the thief across Missouri and found him outside Kansas City. Cole had shot both the thief and the man he had thought was the thief's partner—only to find out it was the man's wife.

Guilty or not, Cole was still haunted by the sight of that long, red braid in the dust.

It was terrible proof of how far he'd fallen. Proof he was no longer the man he'd been before the war—the gentleman farmer who'd never dreamt of violence. Never imagined how much blood would one day cover his hands.

And that was why he didn't just pull his guns now and demand answers from Jimmy. Someone always got hurt when guns were pulled.

But if Mrs. Hurst had had a hand in hurting Steven, then it was up to God to have mercy on her soul, because he would not.

The sight of that bloodstain on the porch would not leave his mind. Something terrible had happened here, and recently. And the way the Hursts pretended that all was fine made him deeply suspicious.

He wore his guns to the dinner table.

"Your sister will not be joining us?" he asked.

"Oh, no, she is caring for Jacks. He appears to have been wounded on the ride." She said it with a smile, as if she had no idea how a man's spurs worked.

"She's better out there with the horses," Jimmy said. "Half animal herself."

Cole was watching Mrs. Hurst and he did not see any betrayal of emotion. No flash of pride or defense. Nothing but that cool smile.

An incredibly convincing liar. Or . . . she was just that cold.

"It's been a long time since we've fed a guest." She sat down on the other stump used as a chair and picked up her own fork and knife.

"He's not a guest." Jimmy's lips and chin were shiny; he was already half through his steak. The level of whiskey in the bottle at his elbow was going down after every bite.

"That's right," she said, bright as day, as if immune to the tensions at the table. "An oil prospector. I must confess I've never heard of the profession. Is that interesting work?"

Cole had no idea. He'd been a farmer, soldier and a bounty hunter—but never a prospector. The only reason he was one now was because that's what Jimmy had been looking for in Denver and that's how he could get onto the land without pulling his guns.

Once he got his answers about Steven, he could kill this man and put his guns away forever.

"Your work must have taken you to some wonderful places," she said when he didn't answer.

He had not been to anyplace wonderful. Not for many years.

"Well." She still talked despite his silence. He was making her efforts at conversation nearly impossible. His sister, if she were alive and here, would kick his shins under the table. "Everyone talks about gold and silver; I had no idea rock oil was out here, as well."

"Not as profitable as gold and silver, so most people don't care." His voice was rough from disuse. He cleared his throat.

She blinked, as if surprised he could speak. "Well, still, it is a treat to have you here."

He laughed down at his plate, taken sideways by her flattery. It had been a very long time since he'd sat down to a table with a lady. And he'd thought his manners and charm long gone, but he was surprised to find them, shabby and rusty, but intact nonetheless.

"You have a poor idea of treats, if I am to be considered one."

"Oh?" She tilted her head, the blond hair gleaming in the firelight. "And what would you consider a treat?"

"A plum. A fresh one."

Her laughter was bright; it brought his head around with surprise. When was the last time he'd heard a lady laugh? "I feel the same way about peaches," she said. "There are days I think I could cry for missing—"

Jimmy's hand snaked across the table to grab her wrist. She did not flinch or wince, her smile was intact, but she went pale, her lips tight. She glanced down at the table and her eyelids fluttered.

He was hurting her.

Cole's hand slipped under the table toward his Colt.

"It's nice, ain't it?" Jimmy asked, his eyes trained on Cole.

"What is?" Cole asked.

"My wife's voice. Reminds me of home. She used to play piano. Had all the boys in knots, lining up to turn the music pages while she played."

Jimmy let go of Mrs. Hurst's wrist and she put her hands in her lap, her smile trembling at the edges. This was the first and only sign that the tensions around the table were affecting her. Evidence that she was not what she seemed, other than a very good actress.

His relief was a faint echo of pleasure.

He did not want to kill her.

"More beans," Jimmy said, and Mrs. Hurst jumped from her chair to get the pot.

"So, you think there's oil here?" Jimmy asked Cole.

"There was some found in Canon City in '62, and there are seeps all over this area."

"I heard the army is paying top dollar."

"Crude sells for six dollars a barrel in Denver." And that was the extent of what he knew about rock oil.

Jimmy smacked his hand down on the table, and Mrs. Hurst flinched so hard she brushed her hand over the hot pot and hissed in pain. Jimmy did nothing, but returned to eating with a certain gleam in his eye as he watched her suffering.

Cole stood from the table. "You all right?"

"Fine," she said, turning away from him as far as she could. "Fine."

"Perhaps if you let me—"

"She said she's fine!" Jimmy barked, his mean eyes only meaner after the whiskey. The brand the home guard had given him was seared right across the corner of his eye and cheek. It was amazing he'd kept his eye at all. The war had changed a lot of things and Cole wondered how this woman, with her china skin and ruined ball gown, had ended up with this man, who clearly relished her pain.

And then he told himself he didn't want to know.

Everyone had their misery. This was hers.

"You a Yankee?" Jimmy pointed his fork at Cole. Cole had seen more than his share of men who still carried the war with them, constantly spoiling for a fight. Jimmy was nothing new.

"I was a soldier."

"From where?"

"West Virginia."

"The Georgia Fifth Infantry." He pointed to his cheek. "This is what I got for my trouble."

"That's what you got for leaving before the end," Cole said. "I was in Georgia. I saw my share of home guard brands."

The woman put the pot down to cool away from the fire and stepped from the table as if getting out of range. She had good survival instincts, he'd say that for her.

"The war is over," she said from the shadows. "Oil, gold, silver, it does not care which side you fought for."

Jimmy stared at Cole. "You agree with that?"

"We all lost enough."

After a long moment Jimmy grunted and went back to his whiskey.

The animosity seemingly settled, Mrs. Hurst returned to the fire. Crouching, she bent her head and Cole felt an odd inclination to rest his hand against her neck, at her shoulder where her hair curled against the faded red of the dress she wore.

It's all right, he would say. *You survived.*

"I don't know." Jimmy leaned back in his chair. He pushed away the plate but pulled the whiskey closer. His eyes were locked on his wife's back, as if he could see that she was bothered, and that weakness incited his blood lust.

The genial tone of his voice was poisonous and the tension around the table was thicker than the steak. Cole leaned back from the table, his hand back on his gun. "I got myself a fine bride and a couple of quality horses. And her sister is a hard worker, only reason to keep her around. So I can't say as I did too badly, did I, Melody?"

She turned, smiling as if he were talking about someone else.

"But Melody." Jimmy shook his head. "She lost it all. Parents, dead. Brother, dead. Fiancé, dead. Land ruined and sold off."

"And yet, here I am," she said, lifting her hands as if she stood in paradise. "Others are not so lucky."

"I'll drink to that," Jimmy said and took a long pull from the bottle.

"This is a pretty piece of property," Cole said. "How long you been settled here?"

"A year," Jimmy answered, but Cole was watching the woman, who jerked at the question, her back stiff with fear. Jimmy was lying.

"Indian trouble?"

"Some Utes, but they been moved west for the most part."

"You plan on farming?"

"Not if you do your job and find the oil."

"I'll do my job." *I will shoot you through your black heart.*

"I'm going to go check on my sister," Mrs. Hurst said, picking up her own plate and adding more beans and steak to it. "Take her some dinner."

"Tell her to stay there tonight," Jimmy said. "We don't need no company in the cabin."

Mrs. Hurst's face went red at the implied message before she nodded and slipped out the door like a ghost.

CHAPTER 4

ONCE SHE WAS outside Melody took great breaths of air to try and settle her stomach, but it didn't work. Nothing would work. The simmering violence around that table had tied her in knots no amount of cold air would untie. Her wrist ached and she was sure Cole Smith was lying about more than just his name. Was there even such a thing as an oil prospector?

The war had taught her to be distrustful and perhaps it was the fact that he did nothing to try and engage her trust that left her off-balance. His poor conversation and rusty flirtation had done nothing to hide his suspicion.

Of Jimmy. Of her. Of the lies they told.

And suddenly she had the perception of that dark-eyed stranger, wearing his guns to the table, as being so much better than her. Lifted to heights simply by not trusting that part she'd played with such brittle and terrified force.

An act she'd nearly dropped when Jimmy had said *We don't need no company in the cabin tonight.*

Most nights, in the year since her wedding night, she'd managed to ply her husband with enough liquor—and sometimes laudanum—that any thought of bedding her was drowned.

But it would seem her reprieve was over.

"Annie," Melody whispered as she stepped into the barn, which appeared empty. She glanced behind her, half afraid that Jimmy or Cole had followed. But there was just the dark night behind her and the cabin across the clearing. "I'm alone."

"Good." Annie's voice came from the cave.

Melody ducked into the cave to see Annie sitting beside Mr. Baywood. The lamplight was reflected on the stone walls and across the spring. He kicked at his blankets, thrashing against Annie where she held him.

"Oh, no," Melody whispered. "Does he worsen?"

"No. I think he's waking up."

Melody groaned, falling to her knees beside her sister. "We do not need this complication."

"What happens inside the cabin?"

"The prospector is not who he says he is," she whispered. "And I really don't think we should underestimate him."

"What do we do?" Annie asked.

Jimmy. Mr. Baywood. The prospector. The specter of what Jimmy wanted to do to her. She could not handle all of these problems. But one of them—the worst of them—she could delay.

"Let me have a dose of laudanum," Melody said. "I'll put it in Jimmy's whiskey. And tomorrow, while Jimmy sleeps, we will send the prospector on his way."

"Do you think that will work?"

"We've drugged him before."

"Not that, sending the prospector away. Will that work?"

"Can you think of something else?"

"I can give you something to kill Jimmy tonight," Annie said. "And we'll be done with the whole business."

Yes! she thought, and not for the first time in her marriage. She was bloodthirsty and terrified, and she could not pretend that the thought of Jimmy dead didn't fill her with a panicked relief. But she shook her head.

I will not make my sister a killer. I won't.

She thought of the way she'd considered that stranger at her table, with his guns and his cold eyes and his obvious lies, as better than her. How much lower did she have to sink? Could she sink?

Hate exploded out of her. Hate for that damn war. Hate for every man that left her to go fight it. Hate that Jimmy had turned her into this creature that lived in such a dark cage of fear, cringing and stooping because she couldn't remember how else to live.

Hate for herself because she suffered it. Day after day.

She blinked away furious tears, because this hate wouldn't solve anything. It only made things worse. It made her defiant when she needed to be acquiescing, and it clouded her thinking when she needed to be clear.

"What if the prospector tries to wake Jimmy tomorrow? What further problems will be created by the prospector realizing he's dead? What if Jimmy owes him money? What if . . . "

"No. You're right. Yours is a good plan."

Good plan was a stretch. There were plenty of places this plan could fail her. Or she could fail the plan, and in not one of those places did she escape the consequences.

Annie reached into the medical bag and pulled out the brown bottle. "Use it all," she said. "He will not die, but it will work quickly."

Melody took the bottle and hugged her sister hard. "Try and keep him quiet," she said. "The last thing you need is the prospector investigating a man shouting in the barn."

Melody felt Annie smile against her shoulder.

After a deep breath, in which she thought all manner of cowardly thoughts, Melody pulled herself away and got to her feet, leaving the barn.

The moon was distant in a cold black sky.

Who was I to come to this? Drugging a man, contemplating murder.

Lying and stealing and calling it survival. Her stomach trembled inside of her skin. *Was I so sinful? My crimes of pride and vanity so great that this is the price?*

She skirted the garden, unable to believe that they had been planning it just that morning. It had felt so good to be at the birth of something.

And now she had to talk her sister out of murder.

"Mrs. Hurst?" His voice came out of the darkness like a gunshot, and she flinched, stumbling.

"Mr. Smith," she whispered, her hand at her throat where her heartbeat pounded. In her other hand she clenched the bottle of laudanum, wishing it were a gun. "You startled me."

"I apologize." He stepped closer, a shadow made real, and she couldn't breathe.

"Do you need anything?" she asked, unable to keep her voice calm.

"No . . . I was just looking at the moon."

"It seems very far away here, doesn't it?"

Shadows fell and retreated across his face as he glanced at the house, and the silence stretched so thin, so painfully thin, she cleared her throat just to break it. "He's had a lot to drink," Cole said. "And his mood is…unsure."

He's worried. About me.

Her vision glittered and her lungs shook as she finally forced herself to suck in a breath. She had to turn away from him, from the temptation of his worry. His concern. There had been a time when she'd had no serious worries of her own. Her father, her brother, Christopher—they'd taken care of her. All she'd had to worry about was how to best reflect them.

What a simple creature she'd been.

And, oh, to be such a simple creature again.

"Thank you," she said, her voice shaking because she was unable, here in the dark, to clutch it all to her chest. "But I will be fine. I do not need you to save me, Mr. Smith." She said his name with every bit of doubt she had about its authenticity.

She felt him as she walked past, the animal heat of him in the cool dark.

JIMMY SAT WITH his feet on the hearth, the bottle of whiskey on the table beside him, surrounded by the dirty dishes. Her hands were suddenly slick around the laudanum; if he caught her trying to dose him . . . She shook her head of the thought before she lost her nerve entirely.

He stared into the fire, and under the guise of cleaning up she walked behind him, pulling his whiskey bottle closer to her. Carefully, silently, she pulled the cork from the laudanum bottle and poured a thin stream into the whiskey.

"What happened to Baywood?" he asked.

"He died. At night on the . . . on the second day. Annie and I buried him in the woods."

Jimmy smiled into the flames.

"What do you think of our oil prospector?" Jimmy asked, reaching for the bottle without looking. Melody jerked sideways, out of the way of his hands. She pushed the whiskey toward him and began to gather the dishes, hiding the laudanum. There had only been time to get about half into the whiskey.

"What do you mean?"

"Don't pretend you wasn't flirting, Melody. I watched you flirt with my brother for years, I know what it looks like."

"It was conversation."

He glanced back at her and then into the fire. He tipped the bottle to his lips and guzzled. The knots in her stomach doubled and redoubled.

"Mama used to say you wasn't good enough for Chris. That you was a slut set out to trap him."

She wished she had the courage to tell him he could not wound her with his words. She knew who she'd been and she did not care what he thought. But her opinions about him, should they be spoken, were not met kindly. Early in the marriage she'd learned at least that much self-preservation.

"Come over here, slut," he murmured, the intent in his voice unmistakable. The fork she used to scrape what little food was left into the scraps bucket for the goat clattered to the ground from her shaking fingers and her head went cold.

"Let me finish cleaning up." She managed to make it sound flirtatious, all the while her heart pounded in her head, in her stomach, her throat.

I hate you. I hate you. I hate you.

"You're mine, Melody. Mine. My brother, all them other fine boys you picked over me, they're dead. And I'd remind you of that fact."

She put down the plates and turned to him. His face was slack in the firelight.

It won't be that bad. Each time since her wedding night had been less . . . bloody. She wouldn't fight. She would think of the garden. The seeds she and Annie had brought west. The rose bush root balls wrapped in burlap. She would think of next summer's pink blooms.

He took another heavy drink of the whiskey and she fought the urge to ask for some for herself. But being drugged was like closing her eyes—it only made opening her eyes harder. He wrapped his fist in her dress, pulling her against him.

No. The thought was a scream in her head. *No! No! No! No!*

His hand slipped; his chin fell to his chest. His eyes closed and then popped open. The drink, perhaps the laudanum, were pulling him under. Relief buckled her knees.

"Let me help you to bed," she said, praying that she had gotten enough into him. And that combined with the whiskey it would do the job.

"What did you do?" His eyes narrowed, his wet lips curled.

"I did nothing."

"We . . . we talked about you lyin' to me." He got to his feet, leaning hard against the table. "What did you do?"

"Nothing," she said, clutching the laudanum, trying to hide it in her skirts.

"Liar," he said and lunged forward. She realized what he was about and tried to duck out of the way, but she was too late.

His fist caught her on the side of the face and she crashed against the hearth before falling to the ground. In blackness.

CHAPTER 5

"I DON'T LIKE this, Duke," Cole whispered, leaning against a fallen pine, the worn leather of his saddle against his back. The stars were scattershot across the dark sky and it had been a long two hours of thinking about how ashamed of him his mother would be.

Duke huffed a deep breath into Cole's ear, and he reached up to scratch at his horse's nose. He should have shot Jimmy on the way up from Denver, because if there was ever a man who needed to be shot, it was Jimmy.

But he needed Steven's letters. He needed whatever information Jimmy had about his brother.

And so he'd let that woman walk into the house, knowing that whatever happened to her, a good part of it was his fault.

He'd been flirting with her. Charmed despite himself.

Cole pushed himself to his feet just as the front door opened and Mrs. Hurst came out. Her hair had come down in pieces, long blonde ropes falling to her waist.

The hair on his own body stood in warning. Her dishabille seemed a terrible sign of violence.

Her back to him, she quietly shut the door and stepped down the small porch. He caught her at the edge of the freshly dug earth.

It had all the makings of a kitchen garden, and his heart was thick with memory. The kitchen garden at home had been turned into a graveyard, full of Union soldiers.

"Mrs. Hurst."

She stopped, her hair, nearly white in the starlight, covering her face. She was as still as a rabbit sensing trouble.

"I am just checking on my sister." She did not look at him.

"Mrs. Hurst." He kept his voice low and quiet and patient. It had been a useful voice for talking pistols away from terrified flag bearers who could march no more into battle.

"Please . . . Go back to your camp. Or better still, go back to Denver. I am sure if you were to find oil, my husband would find a reason to kill you. Saddle your horse and ride away from here."

"Mrs. Hurst." He was a step from her and he could see her shaking so hard the hem of her dress trembled. Her hair trembled. He reached out a hand to her elbow, but she turned, smacking it away.

Half of her face was red and swollen. Her lip was cut.

But her eyes were wild and he took a step away, pushed back by the wrath on her face.

"I remind you of home, don't I? Of your life before this war? My conversation brings back memories of a better time. A better life. A girl, perhaps? Well, that life was a tragedy! It is in ruins, Mr. Smith. As am I." Her voice cracked but her eyes were stone cold. "Go, before my husband wakes and kills us all."

She lifted her skirts and ran. If a trail of smoke had risen from the ground as she passed, he would not have been surprised.

Mrs. Hurst . . . Melody . . . was no accomplice in her husband's masquerade. That was clear. And at this point she would no doubt fully endorse his means of questioning Jimmy about his brother.

Cole glanced at the still, dark cabin and then at the barn, where Melody had run.

He followed her footsteps into the barn.

"HE'S AWAKE?" MELODY hissed, on her knees beside her sister in the cave.

"Light a lamp." The thick male voice came out of the darkness, and Melody pressed her hands to her lips.

"How long?" Melody asked, and could feel her sister's vibrating tension beside her.

"I am lying right here," the voice said again.

"Ten minutes, hard to say," Annie said, and then the lamp wick caught in a bright flare. Annie turned it down as low as she could, and the cave was illuminated by a small orb of light.

Mr. Baywood sat up against the stone wall. The swelling was gone around his forehead—though the bruising remained—and his eyes were clear. She tried not to look below his neck. His chest was . . . large.

"Mr. Baywood—"

"Steven."

"Steven . . . you are alive," she gasped, amazed for the moment that they had done it. They had saved this man. She grabbed her sister in her arms. "You did this. You saved him!"

Annie's lips were trembling and she reached for Melody's face. Belatedly, Melody jerked back, scurried for the shadows.

Annie followed her, guilt writhing in her expression.

"What happened to your face?" Mr. Baywood . . . Steven asked.

"I am fine. Fine. He just . . . hit me before he passed out," she whispered to Annie, ignoring the man who seemed to fill out his body in a way he hadn't while unconscious. How outrageous that they had dragged him to this cave. They must have been possessed by the strength of ten men. "He's still asleep. I think . . . I think we should saddle our horses and ride away."

"I think we should shoot him where he sleeps," Steven said. "Bring me a gun and I will do it myself."

"You can barely sit upright," Melody snapped. "The prospector is leaving. If we hurry we could travel with him."

"What about him?" Annie pointed to Steven. Who was now pushing himself up higher against the cave wall, even though he was sweating and weak.

"We will leave him food and a gun. He can manage."

Annie's gasp of censure was loud in the cave.

"We must care about ourselves now, Annie!" she hissed. "Enough of your Christian kindness! It will get us killed. We must leave."

"Mrs. Hurst?" It was Cole's voice and he was in the barn.

Annie nearly dove for the lamp, extinguishing the flame. Melody pressed her fist to her chest, praying he had not seen the flame reflected on the rock. Praying he could not hear the mad thump of her heart.

"Mrs. Hurst, I mean you no harm." She could hear the prospector's boots against the packed dirt of the barn floor. "I understand your distrust. I am not a prospector. I am searching for my brother—"

Steven made a heavy noise, as if he'd been punched in the chest. Melody crouched beside him, to put her hand over his foolish stupid mouth, but he grabbed her hand in his.

"Cole?" he asked, in a loud, clear voice, and Melody jerked her head sideways, though she could not see Steven.

"Steven?" Cole's voice rang out with sudden urgency.

"Beside the goat. There is an entrance to a cave." Steven turned to Annie. "Light the lamp."

Annie did, with a flint and straw just in time to see Cole walk in through the rocks, his black eyes wide with astonishment. When he saw Steven, he stumbled forward as if his knees were not working. And then they weren't. Cole fell to the ground, his fists clutching the dirt.

Annie stood to face Cole and Melody shook free of

Steven's hands to do the same.

"You will not hurt him," Melody said, with no weapon to back her up. But she had not saved this man only to have him shot again.

"Of course not," Cole whispered, his eyes traveling over Steven's prone body. The light was unreliable but she wondered if there weren't tears in his eyes.

Melody's head was ringing like a bell. She put a hand against the wall to brace herself.

Cole was beside Steven in a blink, his hand going to his blond head, as if to be sure he was real. His fingers shook as they touched Steven's hair and face. And those were tears in his eyes. Annie scrambled to her side and they clung to each other's hands, staring at the men in shock.

"Hello, brother," Cole whispered.

"Took you long enough," Steven whispered, and the two of them smiled. Gently, carefully, Cole bent his head to rest his forehead against his brother's.

Melody turned her eyes from the tenderness. The sweetness between them.

"This is not how I expected to find you," Cole said, glancing over at Annie and Melody against the cave wall.

"They saved my life," Steven said.

"Jimmy would have taken it?" Cole asked, all of his sharp edges on display. He was fierce and quiet. Intent. Utterly terrifying.

"We have an unfortunate history."

Cole braced his hands against hard thighs and stood, facing her.

For some reason, she got the sense that he would touch her. Or was about to, and she pulled away, pressing harder into the stone wall. Not because she was afraid of him, though she was, but because she could not bear to be touched. Not at all. His brown eyes fell from hers and returned to his brother.

"I'll be right back and then let's get you out of this cave."

What . . . what was happening? She could not keep up with how quickly everyone seemed to be moving. Annie crouched and began to gather up her supplies, putting them back into Father's medical kit.

"How did you manage to get me out here?" Steven asked.

"Truthfully," she whispered, "I have no idea."

Cole came back into the cave. "Jimmy is still passed out. You must have dosed him with something?"

"Laudanum," she said, wishing she had some of it for herself. Dreamless sleep would be a blessing.

"Well." Cole smiled at his brother. "Let's get you out of here."

"What about Jimmy?" Melody asked.

"I will take care of Jimmy," Cole said and began to carefully help his brother to his feet.

I will stay here, Melody thought. *I will stay here because I am out of bravery. I have nothing left.* She wanted to cower against these stone walls, press her bruised face to the cold water and let time pass her right on by.

Cole and Steven stepped out of the cave and she turned to Annie.

The question in Annie's eyes was the same one that pounded in Melody's heart.

What will happen to us?

Melody could not let herself die and rot and turn to dust in this cave.

She grabbed Annie's hands. "We will be fine. As long as we are together."

COLE CAREFULLY SETTLED his brother on the ground, propped up against his own saddle. The darkness of the night was just beginning to turn in the east. Dawn was coming.

"What have you heard from everyone? Mother?" Steven asked. His weight was heavier, his voice slurred. The strength gained by their reunion had run out.

"We can talk about this later," Cole said.

Steven's sigh was heavy with knowledge. Duke came over to snuffle around Steven's hair.

"That's Duke." Cole grabbed a shirt from his saddlebags and pulled it over Steven's head.

"You named your horse after your dog?" Steven groaned, lifting his arms through the wide linen sleeves. "How like you, Cole."

Cole didn't know what that meant anymore. *How like you.* That boy he'd been was a stranger. A character in a story he'd heard once, a long time ago, and only dimly remembered.

"I'm going to wait for him on the porch," Cole said, ignoring Steven. "I'll leave you my rifle and pull him out—"

Steven shook his head. "I'm too weak to hold a rifle. I can't take him, even with a clear shot."

Cole looked down hard at his brother and saw him as he was, wounded and impossibly, painfully old, but also the kid, the big brother who led him further and further up the tree. And then helped him down when he got too scared to climb down by himself.

Steven, as he sat in this clearing, was a man defeated. And Cole never thought he'd see that.

"Maybe you should give the gun to the blonde," Steven said. "She probably has a few reasons to put a bullet in Jimmy's head."

On the other side of the clearing, the two women come out of the barn. He could barely see them in the darkness, but the pale gleam of their skin gave them away. Mrs. Hurst glowed in the dawn.

"Melody," Cole said.

"Pardon?"

"Her name is Melody."

They came out from under the trees into the meadow. Her hair was pinned back up, and even from this distance he could see the bruise on the side of her face, the swelling and the cut.

The bump on the opposite temple. It looked obscene.

Cole had learned his lesson in the last six years. The horrors of the world no longer surprised him, but looking at her face, that perfection blighted and ruined, he was shocked by his anger, the icy cold rage on her behalf and at himself for his role in her getting that bruise.

It had been two years since he cared about anything but finding what was left of his family. Caring about Jimmy's soon-to-be widow was uncomfortable. Like sensation returning to a frostbitten toe. Painful and hot.

From inside the cabin there was a thump and a shout, and it was as if even the birds stopped moving.

"Melody! You bitch!" Jimmy yelled, and Cole watched as Melody picked up her skirts and ran across the clearing toward Cole and Steven.

Cole drew his Colt just as she arrived, panting, at his side. He met the eyes in that ravaged face and saw a depth of anger he understood all too well. This woman had been robbed—by the war, the world, but specifically the man inside the cabin.

"Have you ever fired a gun?" he asked.

She nodded, her blue eyes wide.

He handed her the pistol. For a moment he thought she would push it back at him.

But the front door of the cabin opened and Jimmy was belched out, wild eyed and disheveled. "Did you run off, whore?"

Fury, not fear, rolled off of her in a wave and Cole felt the hair rise up on his arms.

"It kicks. Use both hands," he told her. He helped her lift her arm, felt the steadiness of her muscles under the tremble of her skin.

Listening to him, she gripped the gun with both hands, braced herself straight down to the earth, and when Jimmy turned toward her she fired.

The first shot missed, but the next three didn't.

She blew the bastard right off the porch.

The boom of the pistol shots echoed throughout the clearing. Animals in the underbrush scattered and his ears rang in the silence that followed.

"Lord forgive me," she whispered, sinking to the ground, her skirts billowing up around her. He grabbed his Colt before she hurt herself.

Annie ran up and fell to her knees beside her sister.

Leaving them, Cole went to see Jimmy where he lay bleeding into the dirt, his eyes wide open in a death stare. She'd hit his stomach, his chest and his neck.

Cole looked at the gun in his hand and threw it onto the porch.

I am done with you.

CHAPTER 6

COLE BURIED JIMMY in the forest. Melody wanted him to be left out for the creatures. She wanted birds to pull out his eyes, wolves to tear apart his flesh. But Cole didn't want those animals close to the barn.

I shot him. I shot my husband. A man I've known since he was a boy following his brother to school.

She tried, after the initial shock wore off, to feel more guilt, but she didn't.

And that terrified her. Was she so dead inside that she couldn't even feel remorse for her soul? Was she so numbed, so hardened by her treatment at his hand that she couldn't ache for things to be different?

But she didn't.

He was dead and she'd killed him. Shot him.

And she'd never dreamed, *never dreamed* that she'd be capable of that. That she would *want* that bloody end for him at her hands.

But Cole had taken one look at her and pressed that gun into her hand.

What had he seen in her that made him do that? How had he known? She felt naked, somehow, when he looked at her. As if he could see something far more shocking than the edge of her petticoat.

Parts of her she didn't even realize she had were revealed. To him.

Melody cleaned up the cabin, erasing any sign of Jimmy. And then she pulled his saddlebags onto the porch, sat, and salvaged what little clothing he had. What couldn't be saved would make rags. Annie was checking Steven's wound and Cole was still in the forest.

Her face pounded, her ribs ached, but the laudanum was all gone. The bottle had shattered against the table when she fell.

"Mrs. Hurst." Cole's voice snapped her head up and she winced at the pain radiating down her neck.

"Call me Melody," she said. "I have no fondness for Mrs. Hurst."

Cole's smile was brief, but surprising. His teeth were very white.

"You buried him?" she asked.

Cole put the spade against the porch and sat down, leaning against the pine trunk that made up the beam. She felt herself swimming in the air.

"I did. You really should sleep, Melody."

She looked at him. There were two and then there were three and finally there was one of him again.

"I miss playing the piano," she said. "I miss my mother. I miss garden parties and dancing. I was a very good dancer."

"I think you've hurt your head worse than you might have thought."

"What do you miss?"

"There's nothing left to miss. I found my brother."

He was lying. She'd seen it in his face when he handed her the gun. He had a well of grief inside of him. A black anger over all he'd lost. It was something they shared.

She sighed, looking over at Steven and Annie. Annie pulled a blanket up on Steven's chest and sat back. Then she took off her glasses to better dig at her eyes.

"My sister saved his life," she said. "She pulled out that bullet with her own hands."

"I am grateful."

She turned her head, lost him for a moment but found him again. He'd taken off his hat and dark hair stuck to his forehead in clumps. Over and over again she'd watched her mother brush the hair off her father's head. He'd had a cowlick, right in the middle, and Mother would lick her fingers and pat it down before company came over.

"Are you grateful enough to be kind?" she whispered. "I miss kindness. I miss it most of all."

COLE STARED AT his brother, sleeping beside the fire inside the cabin. The flames gave his Viking looks a gentle expression. The blond bear, that's what they used to call him. The great blond bear. Cole wanted to wake his brother up and ask him if he remembered convincing Gavin that if he took the boat to the middle of the pond during a full moon, the fish would jump into the boat by the dozens. Of course, when Gavin got stuck out in the middle of the pond, the oars sinking to the bottom, Steven had been the one to swim out and tow him back. Did he remember tricking their sister into sleeping with yarrow under her pillow so she would dream of her true love, only to wake up hysterical and covered in hives? Father had given him a proper lashing for that one, not that it changed Steven at all.

Nothing changed Steven—there was no consequence that could be applied to his actions that would make him turn course.

"You never learn," their mother had despaired, to which Steven had laughed and replied, "Who wants to?"

Steven shifted on his bedroll, the nightmare coming upon him again. "Yes," he mumbled. "Yes! Of course, son. Of course. Yes!" He was yelling, and Cole slipped to the wooden edge of the shelf where Steven slept to wake his brother. "I will tell her. She will know, I swear it. I will go to her myself. It's all right. You were a good soldier. A good boy."

"Steven," Cole said, giving him a small shake. Steven awoke on a gasping breath. His eyes wild, but his body eerily still.

"Where are the guards?" he whispered.

"There are no guards." Under his hands Steven's skin was clammy. Slick. "You are in your cabin. Far away from Andersonville."

His brother's face melted with relief before he sagged back onto the thin linen mattress with the blankets of his bedroll spread across it.

"Cole," he whispered. His smile was a shadow of what it had been in their youth. Ask anyone and they would say that Steven was the fun one. Always laughing. There was not much sign of laughter anymore. But his hand, familiar and rough, grabbed Cole's and held on hard, as if Cole had come at just the right moment to save him from drowning. "I keep thinking this is a dream I'll wake up from."

Cole pushed Steven's sweaty hair from his face, as Mother would have done. "I'm here. Are you hungry? I've heated the beans and venison from last night."

"No. Thirsty, though."

Cole got Steven to sit up against the wall and brought him a full tin cup. Steven's cup was from the First Virginia Volunteer Infantry Regiment. The moment of opportunity, Steven had signed up for his chance at glory.

Cole remembered all the girls from town waving their handkerchiefs at him as he left.

Cole had taken more time. Joining the Northern Army months later. And only Jane, Mother and Samantha waved goodbye.

They never fought together. Not once. And for that Cole was grateful. He'd seen enough men die while he'd marched and marched, unscathed, through battle after battle. There had been nightmares of seeing Steven or Gavin fall, shot full of lead, bones turned to powder, intestines to liquid, all while he marched past, stuck in formation.

"Careful," Cole said, helping his brother drink.

"I'm so weak." Steven wiped his lips with a shaking hand.

"You've been unconscious for over a week, I'm told."

Cole sat back at the table. The cabin smelled like his tobacco and the beans and steak he had eaten. The two women slept in the room on the other side of the fireplace.

The house was full and lived-in tonight and Cole found himself pushing at his own shrunken, miserly edges. Mrs. Hurst . . . Melody . . . had asked him what he missed from life before the war and he hadn't answered. But the truth was this. He missed family in a house. Together.

"Who was Hurst to you?" He asked.

"A guard at Andersonville. He helped me escape."

"Why?"

"I paid him. Money was easier to get in prison than fresh water."

Andersonville—the thought of that camp made his blood cold. The thought of his brother there made him want to weep. The fire crackling was the only sound for long moments.

"Why did he shoot you?"

"After he helped me escape, I had told him we'd travel together so if anyone caught us he could say he was taking me back to prison. It wasn't the best lie, but if he was smart about it, most soldiers would've believed it. The war was almost over, most men were tired of killing. But once we started traveling, he was lazy and stupid and I knew if I stayed with him, we'd both be caught. So I left him. He must have been caught by the home guard not long after."

"But you made it all the way to Virginia?"

"I made it home, as much as is left of it."

Cole had made it home, too, or to the scarred and burnt earth where their home used to be. There was little left to salvage and he had not had the heart to try without his family, so Cole had left the land for the crows.

"How long were you in Andersonville?" he asked. "How did you get—"

Steven shook his head, his eyes on the fire. "Let's not speak of it, Cole. I would rather be glad you're here than think of that place."

Cole nodded. He understood the way some things were too awful to put words to.

Andersonville, by all accounts, was just such a place.

"It's a miracle I found you," he said. "Hurst took almost all the letters, and if it hadn't been for that scar I don't know that I would've been able to track him."

"Some nights," Steven said, "I would think how unlikely it all was. That any of you survived, or got my first letter, or would follow me to St. Louis and receive the other letters."

"It was a good thing you left three letters in St. Louis."

"I left one for you, one for Gavin and one for Samantha in every city."

"Sam is dead."

There was nothing to do but tell him, though he could have been kinder. But he'd forgotten how to be kind. There'd been no need for it in the last few years.

Steven sucked in a deep breath, as if they were all at the pond again and Gavin and Cole had both tried to put him under water. "Gavin?"

"I haven't heard, but…"

"Me neither."

"Mother's gone, too."

Steven's face curled in on itself and he lifted his hand to his face to hide his eyes. The tears. Cole stared into the fire, his guts so small they could fit in his hand.

"When?"

"Charleston, last year of the war. The letter from Aunt Louisa said it was her heart. And it was fast."

Steven breathed hard through his nose and Cole finally went to sit beside his brother while they grieved, shoulder to shoulder. After a while, Cole thought perhaps Steven had fallen asleep again. But when he turned he found the fire reflected in Steven's open eyes. The unblinking nature of that gaze worried Cole, and he wondered what exactly his brother was seeing in that fire.

"So you're an oil man now?" Cole asked, nudging his brother from his thoughts.

Steven's dry laugh lifted his chest and he winced. "I made the claim, thinking there might be gold, and if I was wrong I'd farm or breed horses, but I found these two seeps and it keeps me busy."

"Is there any real money in that?"

"I sell two barrels of crude in Denver or Pueblo every couple of months. Between that and the trapping, it's enough for coffee and beans with a little extra to put in the bank."

"The bank? You finally stopped spending your money on Alisha Blackstone and her daddy's rotgut whiskey? Mother would be so proud."

Steven's smile was the saddest thing he'd ever seen. "Don't worry. Behind the barn, on the other side of the outcrop, there's another clearing. You can plant all the apple trees you like. We'll drink cider until it comes out our ears."

I don't think I'm that man anymore, he thought.

A log fell in the fire, sending up a shower of sparks.

"What are we going to do with the women?"

Cole sighed. "That is the very same question I've been asking since I rode into the clearing."

"If one of them had pulled the trigger on me . . . ?" Steven's voice was pitched low, though Cole was sure neither of the women on the other side of the wall was awake. It had been a very long day. "What would you have done?"

"Killed them."

Steven flinched and Cole realized how cold he seemed.

How cold he'd become.

"I'm a bounty hunter, Steven. It's what I do. There was no farm to go back to. And I had to keep moving, looking for you. For Gavin." It sounded as if he were trying to convince himself. "I was good at it. The war trained me well."

He could feel his brother staring at him.

"I don't quite recognize you, brother."

Cole met Steven's blue eyes—their mother's eyes. But empty and bleak where they'd once been merry. "I could say the same, brother."

On the other side of the fire, the wall, one of the women rolled over, the rustle of blankets over clothing loud in the silence. A reminder that they weren't alone.

There'd been a boy—Cole couldn't remember his name—just a kid from Virginia, spotty and scared. Every night he'd wake everyone up crying and screaming for his Mama. Some of the men threw things at him, wet socks, hardtack, rocks. But the kid wouldn't shut up. Got so Cole was used to it.

When the boy died, torn to pieces by cannon shrapnel, Cole found the next night he couldn't sleep in the silence. In the silence he realized how badly he missed his own mother. His family. His farm. His goddamned dog. It was if those memories, those feelings had just been waiting for the silence so they could be found.

This moment, his pipe in his hand, his brother at his shoulder, the room warm all around them, he felt the same way.

I will never be alone again.

He bit his lip against sudden tears.

"Maybe they have family they want to get back to," Steven said.

But Melody. Jimmy's words from dinner were a splinter under the surface of his memory. *She lost it all. Her parents, dead. Her brother, dead. Her fiancé, dead.*

"Perhaps," Cole agreed, but he didn't think Melody was

that lucky.

MELODY COULD FEEL her sister breathing in the dark beside her.

"You're not asleep," Annie whispered, her voice pitched so low as to not travel past them. A trick learned in their beds as girls, refined at every chance as they got older.

"No," Melody said, tracking the shadows across the cabin's ceiling.

"You heard?" she whispered.

Melody shook her head; she had not been paying attention to the men's conversation in the far room.

"He would have killed us, Melody." Annie's fear was a palpable thing, reaching cold fingers into the fog occupying Melody's head.

They were at the mercy of two strangers, one of whom handed her the gun with which to kill her husband as if it had been a canteen of water. This should concern her, she knew that.

But she could not feel any more fear. Her seams had torn and all of her fear and all of her worry—they were gone. She simply didn't care.

"I don't know what to do," she whispered, unable to look at her sister.

"I do." Annie grabbed her hands. "I know. For once, I will make the plan. We'll leave."

"We have no money," Melody said. "We've sold everything of value."

"Except the horses."

Melody took a deep, shuddering breath. They'd gone to incredible lengths to keep the stallion and two mares from being conscripted or killed for food. They were the legacy passed down from her mother's family. They were the basis of her family's barn, the best of the stock.

"Lilly will fetch us the most money," Annie said.

"Lilly was Mama's favorite."

"We need money, Melody. This is no time for sentiment."

Of course not. The time for sentiment was years ago. She would sell the horse.

"Where will we go?" Melody asked.

"Denver."

"Opium dens and whore houses? Sounds lovely."

Annie sighed, never fond of Melody's sarcasm when it was a knife wielded against her. "If you had all the money in the world, where would you go?"

"Wherever you wanted."

"Melody—"

"What do you want me to say, Annie? I understand you are trying to make our freedom a great adventure, but the only place I want to be is back on the farm with our family. That's what I want. Home. Everything else is just surviving."

"Jimmy is dead." She said it like that should bring her joy. Comfort. But it didn't.

"Yes, well, that makes surviving more likely, doesn't it?" Melody rolled over. "Your plan is sound. We'll leave for Denver in the morning."

COLE WOKE UP before dawn and quietly stepped out of the house. The June morning was cool and damp. He pulled his hat down low over his ears and turned up the collar on his coat. To his surprise, Melody and Annie were already awake and busy in the clearing.

It appeared they were packing up their horses.

Side by side, the resemblance between them was small. Melody was taller, her body more sturdy, though both women were painfully thin. Annie's features were more refined, Melody's lush. Her eyes wider, her lips fuller.

Annie's brown hair reminded him of his sister's, rather untamable.

Melody's hair was the bright gold of a cavalry braid.

"You're up early," he said, startling both of them. They wore most of their clothing; he could see the hems of multiple dresses at the top of Melody's boots.

"Are you leaving?" he asked, stunned at the thought. The widow looked pale and wan; that bruise on her face was worse this morning than it had been last night.

"That is our plan," Annie said, her brown eyes focused and sharp behind her glasses.

"Are you sure that's wise?" he asked. *Because it is decidedly unwise.*

"We don't wish to burden you," Annie said. Melody was eerily quiet, a shadow standing next to her sister.

"You're no burden, I assure you. My brother needs care that I have no training to provide."

"You keep the wound and bandages clean. Help him regain his strength. He is through the worst of it," Annie said, sounding damnably reasonable.

"But there's too much to be done here for me to care for him."

The sisters shared a dubious look.

"I will pay you, of course," he said.

That changed the nature of the sisters' look.

"Mr. Smith—" Annie said.

"Please. Cole."

"Cole. May I speak freely?"

The events of the past days, he would have thought, put them beyond drawing-room manners. "Please," he said, playing along.

"We heard you last night, speaking to your brother about us."

They heard him say he would have killed them.

His skin prickled as his stomach fell to his boots. His eyes flew to Melody's, but she was seemingly engrossed in brushing her horse's neck. "I'm sorry . . . I didn't intend for you to hear that."

"Obviously," Annie said. "But you can understand our reluctance to stay."

"How much would you pay us to stay and care for your brother?" Melody asked, drawing her sister's angry gaze. There was no sign in Melody of the young, merry hostess she'd been just the other night, or the wild-eyed Valkyrie standing over his brother to keep him safe, or even the soul-dead woman on the porch begging for just a glimpse of kindness. She was cold and distant, buried deep inside herself.

"Ten dollars a week," he answered.

The amount was intended to make it impossible for them to turn it down, and neither of them could quite control the widening of their eyes.

"For how many weeks?" Melody asked.

"Until he doesn't need you any longer, I imagine."

"That's at least two weeks. Perhaps more," Melody said.

Annie was scowling harder at Melody; apparently this was not what the sisters had decided.

"What are you doing?" Annie asked under her breath.

"Earning money so we don't have to sell Lilly," Melody answered.

"On my honor you are safe here," he said to them, ignoring the deep irony of him saying those words to them. Nevertheless, he hoped to tip their doubts into faith.

"On your honor," Melody scoffed, and he let the insult roll off his shoulders.

"If it would put your mind at ease I will camp out of the cabin," he said. "And if I may say, Melody, you are in no shape to ride. You look ready to collapse."

She blushed and pressed her hand to the bruise as if she'd forgotten. Annie came up to stand beside her, her arm around her shoulders.

"My sister and I need to discuss this," Annie said to him.

"Of course." He gave them a little bow, a small relic from the drawing rooms and parlors of his past life, and headed to the barn.

There was a lot of work to do around the property, far more than just daily chores. The barn needed to be bigger. They needed a smokehouse and chicken coop. He needed to investigate these seeps of Steven's and this clearing he claimed would be good for apples.

Before the war, Cole had convinced Father to graft the York Imperial apples with Newtown Pippins, and the cider had been improving. He'd been selling it to the tavern for a handsome profit. Mother had been scandalized, but secretly pleased, and Steven had teased all of them for their merchant instincts.

He closed his eyes against the sharp, bitter pain of those memories. But there were more behind them.

His father walking through the hedgerows at dawn in his tall boots, two dogs at his side, Gavin sprinting ahead.

Samantha weaving crowns of apple blossoms.

Mother's pie.

Oh God. I can't bear it.

If he could bash those memories out of his head, he'd do it to save himself the pain of remembering.

There would be no orchard on this land. Steven had the right idea; they would turn their efforts to oil, because it reminded them not at all of home. He did not have the soul for farming anymore.

Those memories would be starved to death behind stones. He'd give them no air. No room. And when they died, he'd be free again.

Carefully, he gathered warm eggs from beneath disgruntled chickens and tucked them into the pockets of his coat.

When he imagined enough time had passed and the work of the day could no longer be put off, he left the barn and found the women still in conversation beside their horses.

"We've decided that we will stay," Annie said when he was close. "Until Steven no longer needs care, and then we would be obliged if you could see us safely to Denver. We will pay you of course—"

"You will not. I will pay you for saving my brother's life at great risk to your own." He met Melody's gaze, steely and distant. Did she not understand what she'd done for him? What was owed to her? "You speak of kindness, but I can never repay yours. I'm in your debt."

Melody turned away from his gaze. It was obvious Melody didn't trust him; neither of them did.

And he couldn't convince her. Whatever words she needed he didn't have. He had work and memories and four eggs.

"I have gathered breakfast." He patted his pockets. "Come in when you're ready."

He crossed the clearing, his fingers catching the blossoms of the flowers as he walked by, the petals the very same velvet texture of his old dog's ears. He closed his fist around the next blossom and stripped every petal from the stem.

If only memories were so easily destroyed.

CHAPTER 7

ANNIE SPENT THE day being angry and Melody knew well enough to leave her to her sulk. She would get over it in time and see that the plan to stay here and earn money was far wiser than leaving for Denver with nothing.

And they could keep Lilly for just a little while longer.

But until Annie came to see that Melody was right, she huffed around the cabin.

"I think you two are fighting," Steven said when he woke up, groggy and weak.

"You don't fight with your brother?" Melody asked.

"We used to. But with our fists. Far more civilized."

"Sadly, that is not an option for us," Annie said with a look over her shoulder at Melody that declared she was ready to try.

"My sister was good at the silent treatment," Steven said, closing his eyes as Annie unwound the bandages at his waist. "Once she ignored Cole for a whole month."

"He must have done something awful," Annie murmured, checking the pink wound.

"I don't remember." Steven's voice was dry and cracked. "I wish I could."

Melody understood. So many of the good memories had

been crowded out and bullied away by the bad memories.

Tired of the silent tensions in the cabin, Melody left to pick some of the wild onion she'd found behind the barn. Her head felt as if it floated above her body and her arms and legs were longer than they'd been yesterday. Strange.

As she walked past the flowers in front of the cabin, she stopped. How lush they were. A perfect carpet of soft blooms. Before she knew she was doing it, she waded into those flowers and lay down, the stems and leaves cracking under her weight, making a damp blanket between her and the dirt. The crushed blossoms perfumed the air, sweeter than any rose water she and Annie could make. Sweeter than any of the French perfume Daddy had bought for Mama before the war. Above her, the blooms bobbed against a bright blue sky. White clouds sailed past, castles of them, thick and dense and tall.

Look at that, she thought, filled with a quiet wonder, a small trickle of peace, that grew and spread, eroding the walls of fear that she had lived with for so long. Tears burned behind her eyes but she blinked them away, not wanting to be blinded to any of this beauty.

I killed him, she thought, unable to even think his name in this beautiful place in fear he would ruin it. *I won't have to suffer another moment of pain with that man.*

"Melody?" It was Cole, standing over her with a string of trout over his shoulder. "Are you all right?"

How ridiculous to be found here like this, but she couldn't be bothered to care.

I'm free.

"Did you fall?" He glanced over his shoulder, panicked. "Do you need your sister?"

"No," she answered, smiling because she wanted to and not because she was terrified not to. "I'm fine." She flung out her arms, her fingers brushing the soft flower heads, the green damp stems. A honeybee hummed around her head, landed on her finger and buzzed away.

"Melody," he said, all stern concern.

She shook her head at him. "Don't," she said. "I've been living terrified and small for years. But not right now. Right now, I am not scared at all."

Do you understand, she wanted to ask? *Do you understand how beautiful it is to lie here in the dirt and flowers and look at the sky?*

Something happened under the skin of his face, something strange, as if the muscles holding his mouth in stern lines, keeping his eyes narrowed, they all just gave way and she saw for a moment all the fear he still lived with, the heavy weights of grief and regret.

"Do you remember what you were like before the war?" she asked.

He shook his head.

I've only remembered the worst of myself, tracing every moment of bad fortune back to some horrible deed in my past. But there was more to me. I'm sure there was.

The sun gave him a halo. And she had no illusions that he was an angel.

We are all just human, she thought. *Trying to survive.*

She wished he would lie down in these flowers with her. He needed it.

"Come on, Melody," he said, wrapping his hand around hers, his other hand at her waist as he pulled her up out of the grass and flowers. "You should be resting."

Inside Annie clucked over her, their fight forgotten, and Melody was sent to bed.

In the morning they all talked about her head injury and told stories about soldiers they'd known who'd been hit in the head and couldn't remember their names, or could only sing instead of speak.

And she agreed with them. I was not myself, she said.

But she knew the truth.

That was the day she found herself again; like a diamond,

hard and unbroken beneath all the rubble.

MELODY SLEPT. WOKE up and slept all day and the night again. She woke up the following morning to the roar of her stomach and the smell of her body and decided to make biscuits. A lot of them. And then it was time to do some wash. And take a bath.

Steven slept as well, his back turned to the otherwise empty room. After dressing, she grabbed the bucket and went out into the clearing for water. Only to be brought up short by the sight of Cole, to the left of the barn, shirtless and shaving, looking into a mirror propped up in a tree.

His skin was surprisingly dark, stretched taut over thick muscles. He lifted his arms and the muscles in his belly clenched and released. He had hair on his chest and a thin line of it on his belly. He was lean, no fat on him.

There were no scars on his body. He turned away to pick something up from the ground and she saw his back was clear too.

She had not seen a man returned from the war quite so unscathed.

He must have caught sight of her because he grabbed the shirt hanging from a branch and pulled it over his head.

"I didn't see you there, Melody," he said. His face beneath the dripping water was red. He was embarrassed.

You are a man, she thought. The tightening in her stomach, not quite painful, but not at all comfortable, not sexual in any way. Just precisely, exquisitely aware.

Since the war she'd been afraid of men, of the potential threat of them. Just days ago she'd been terrified of this same man, in this same clearing.

But suddenly she remembered *liking* them. Their bodies. Their smiles. The deep timber of their voices. The foreign nature of their masculinity and how it used to make her feel so protected and powerful all at once.

And she was lost somewhere in the awkwardness of his bare chest and her not being afraid. The manners that had ruled her life had long been forgotten, but the survival of the past few years left her with so few graces to navigate this situation.

"I was getting water," she said, lifting the bucket, because she needed to say something.

He nodded.

"The other day—" She pointed to the flowers, where the indentation of her body could still be seen.

His smile was brief and startling, his face transformed. "Before the war that wouldn't have even made me look twice," he said. "My sister was fond of naps in tall grass. It's something I forgot about."

"Me too," she said.

Silence rippled between them. The sun was skewered on the tops of the trees to the east.

"I slept two days away."

"You must have needed it."

"Who knew shooting your own husband could be so exhausting?"

Mama always said her sarcasm was ugly. Made her ugly, and his stunned expression was the proof right now. Mortification burned through her.

"I'm sorry—" she breathed. She was truly not herself and it was alarming to have so little control.

"You shot him three times," he said. "Triple the exhaustion."

Shocked, she laughed, a loud bark that wasn't refined or ladylike or anything but honest. It felt good.

"That explains it." This man standing here with the shy, quiet smile was a far cry from the cold killer she'd first thought him to be. "And you, you must just be tuckered from pretending to be an oil prospector."

"Now that you mention it, I suppose I am."

She narrowed her eyes at him, enjoying the teasing. "Do

you even know anything about oil?"

"Not one thing. I have pretended to be a dentist, a doctor, a railroad man and an oil prospector. I fear since the war all I am is a very good liar. "

"You're not alone," she said, thinking of her many lies. "My mother would not be proud."

His laughter was dark and rich and lovely, but it covered a grief. And perhaps a shame. Same as hers. "Neither would mine," he said.

She smiled at him for too long and he began to clear up his shaving things with hurried hands.

"You...you and your brother must have so much to catch up on," she said, reluctant to see him go. She'd been social before the war, a gossip more than anything, but Jimmy had kept them in hotel rooms and distant camps far away from people for ten months. She missed conversation.

"We do." His smile was a glimpse into a hundred memories, a lifetime of shared moments. "I haven't seen him since the war started. He was the first from our town to volunteer. I wasn't so brave and joined later."

Six years. The thought of those years without her sister was awful. She quite simply would not have survived.

"My sister has been my greatest comfort these last years. I could not imagine not having her by my side."

"It's... it's like losing a little bit of who you are." Cole wiped water from his face. He had a fine chin. Dimpled but strong. And his lips were . . . well, they were lovely. "And there are only the two of us left. My parents, my brother and sister. All gone. If Jimmy had killed Steven . . . " He shook his head as if he just didn't have words for that reality.

Her hands strangled the edge of the bucket. The threadbare charm she wore for Jimmy was nowhere to be found, and she felt naked and raw under Cole's gaze. All she could think of was his face as he handed her that gun. The way he seemed to understand that her soul was less important than killing the man who had taken so much from her.

"I would have shot Jimmy myself," he said softly, as if he could see the place her thoughts had gone. "He was going to die, by your hand or mine, it didn't matter. So if your guilt—"

"I didn't know I wanted that," she whispered, interrupting him. "How did you?"

He blinked, but did not look away. Did not seem discomfited by the sudden familiarity between them. That act—him handing her the gun and her using it to shoot Jimmy—it stitched them together in an ugly violent seam. "I thought you should have the choice."

"Choice?" A raw bubble of mirth exploded from her lips. There had been no choice but survival for many years. And now suddenly she had too much.

Choice was a burden she didn't want to carry.

"My brother and I discussed your intention to leave in two weeks," Cole said. "But my brother has to travel back to Denver to receive a shipment a month from now, which I know extends your stay, but it would save us a trip."

She struggled not to take a giant, relieved breath. A month was a fine reprieve. "I'll have to talk to my sister, but I think that's agreeable."

"Your . . . " he gestured up to his own eye. "Your face looks better. Not so swollen."

"That's too bad, I was thinking of a career on the stage as a monster. Scaring children."

"We'll, we'd better get you back to Denver quick, before it all fades and you are beautiful again." As far as flattery went, she'd had better. Christopher had been silver-tongued. Poetic, nearly, in his appreciation for her hair and eyes and lips. But still she felt a wild, hot blush sweep up her neck and across her cheeks.

She lifted the pail. "I . . . I need to get water. I'm making biscuits."

Cole smiled and there was something boyish in his

expression. Something young and happy. She had not seen that in their short acquaintance and it left her off-balance. "I haven't had biscuits in a long time."

"You shouldn't get your hopes up. I haven't made them in a while. I might have forgotten how."

"I'm sure they'll be wonderful."

"I wish I had some plum preserves to put on them for you."

His surprise should have been embarrassing for both of them. She'd been too forward with her sudden strange consideration. Too eager. But it was only kindness.

Which was why it seemed so odd, because kindness was an animal neither of them had seen in such a long time.

"What are you doing with this land?" Cole pointed to the soil she and her sister had turned what felt like years ago.

The plot was so pretty, a fresh black rectangle in a sea of green. "A kitchen garden. We wanted to grow something," she said. At his silence, she realized how presumptuous that was. And all that embarrassment she refused to feel was a wave sweeping her up.

"I'm sorry," she whispered. The thin cotton of her skirt clung to hands that were suddenly damp. "Truly. Perhaps we could—"

"Put it back?" He laughed and she smiled at the thought. What a surprise this man was. "What were you going to grow?"

"My . . . my sister and I brought seeds from home and gathered more along the way." She could feel him looking at her, the heat of his gaze like the sun against her skin. "Carrots, beets, peas, strawberries, corn. Some fruit trees. Plums, mostly. Peaches."

"Plums," he said. Actually, he nearly gasped.

Her smile was real; she felt its pleasure all through her body. "We will give you a seed to plant. The trees take a long time to grow, but eventually you will have your plum."

"That . . . that is very kind. Once, on the march in Georgia,

I found a jar of plum preserves in a cellar. I ate it with my fingers and nearly cried."

She went cold at his words.

"You marched with Sherman?" she asked, and he stilled as if he realized what he'd done. He'd opened the door everyone preferred would stay shut.

Slowly, he nodded.

"My home was near Savannah."

Sherman's Christmas present to Lincoln.

"I'm sorry." His words were as naked as he'd been when she walked out here. Truly he appeared sorry.

Sorry would not return her life to her. Her mother and father and fiancée. All her uselessness and frivolity. But all of that seemed very far away now. That girl she'd been, that life. It was a dream. She had no more hate and anger to heap upon this man. Perhaps killing Jimmy had lanced that wound; she didn't know and didn't have the energy to care.

"I joined the war believing in something," Cole said. "But, at this moment, I could not tell you what it was."

"You won," she said.

"My father died at Bull Run, my brother and I enlisted with the Union, my younger brother went to the Rebels, and I have heard no word from him since the morning he left. My mother and sister, when the fighting grew too close, went south to Charleston to stay with her people there. I never saw them again. My family's home was burned down, the fields are burial grounds. If that is winning, I can't imagine what losing feels like."

She touched his hand, just above the thumb where there was a dip, a small pocket of skin that was warm and damp, and then she pulled her hand away. Cold comfort perhaps, but all she had.

"Remarkably," she said, "it feels the same."

DAYS PASSED WITH a strange harmony. The kind he'd

never thought to experience again. Cole built the smokehouse and in the dawn hours he hunted and fished to fill it so they would have food over the winter. Melody made the most of what he brought back to the cabin, surprising all of them with what she could do with the wild plants she and Annie found while foraging in the woods.

Steven got stronger, though Annie still clucked over him. Yesterday morning he'd snapped at her to stop touching him. That he needed no more fussing and he could dress his own wounds. Annie had stiffened, her hands pulled away as if she'd accidentally stuck them in a fire. She quit the cabin, mumbling something about finding Melody.

"You could have done that better," Cole said into the silence.

"She touches me too much."

"She's only checking your wounds," Cole said.

Steven didn't answer.

"Are you accusing her of touching you for some other reason?" Cole asked, attempting to tease, but Steven's eyes flared and Cole didn't know what his brother was thinking.

"Whatever her reasons, it's too much," Steven said and rolled over, leaving Cole to wonder how his brother could be right there and at the same time, so distant.

The quiet industry of the four of them working together in that clearing, it reminded him of the very best days with his family. And those memories pressed against his skin, his head, making him ache. Every night, he found himself on his feet after supper, leaving the cabin at twilight as if it were an enemy to run from.

He'd marched for four years as a Union soldier and the war had replaced living and vital flesh with a cancer of memory. And then he'd gone west, eating his own heart so what was left of him wouldn't notice the horrors he was committing in the name of finding his brother.

The countless dead, laid to rest with his hands.

There had been the boy soldiers in the war, with their hairless faces and terrified eyes. His first bounty outside of Independence, a stagecoach robber who'd pissed his pants and begged for his life. The two brothers who'd raped and murdered the mayor's daughter outside of St. Louis. The horse thieves with dead eyes and bad aim. That red braid in the dust.

He'd thought when he found Steven, when he put his guns away, he would find some peace. But apparently, that was not to be.

And Melody. He'd thought, so foolishly that first night with Jimmy and all of her forced and merry conversation, that he'd been charmed by her, by the ray of sunshine her laughter forced into his world. But the sight of Melody lying in those flowers, staring up at the sky as if she'd seen the face of God, that rolled the rock away from his cave and now there was too much light to run from.

And he'd handed her that gun! Given her the opportunity to live as he did, restless and disturbed. Half-human.

She'd actually joked about killing her husband, but he could sense the edge of panic in her and he wondered if she was haunted now. If he'd done that to her, offered her the means with which to gather her own ghosts. He could not bear himself. He spread his own disease without thinking. Without noticing.

One morning, a week after he'd been in the clearing, he and Melody sat on the porch and skinned rabbits, waving away the flies that buzzed around their heads. The fur he would trade when they went to Denver, but he kept some aside for them, thinking of warm, fur-lined gloves for winter.

"My brother was a terrible hunter," she murmured, breaking the thick silence between them. She was smiling. Thinking of her dead brother, her hands covered in blood and gore, and she was smiling. A quiet internal smile, so different than the forced frivolity she'd shown him at first. It was as genuine and real and sweet as anything he'd seen. "Fishing was worse. He couldn't sit still, or stay quiet for longer than a minute. He had the patience of a mayfly. Father got to the point he didn't even try anymore and he started taking Annie with him."

"Was she a good hunter? With her leg?"

"Better than my brother. She could sit still and wait. Without her skill, we would have been far hungrier during the war."

She did this all the time, engaged him in these small conversations as if she were leaving a breadcrumb trail outside his cave to draw him out. And it worked, over and over again it worked, and he found himself talking to her more than he'd talked for months at a stretch.

"Your brother died?" he asked.

"Kernstown."

"First or second?"

"First. Mama died not long after. Went to sleep in her rocking chair and didn't wake up. But it's a relief to me now, thinking of her in heaven with Father and Joel." With the back of her wrist she brushed back a long blonde curl that had fallen over her face. "What about your brother?"

"He's in the cabin."

She leaned over and nudged him with her shoulder. The sensation, heavy and sweet and gone too fast. "Tell me about your other brother. Gavin?"

He shook his head as if he could deny the memories, but then they just came rolling out of that cave, undeniable and real. "He was very patient. Very quiet. An excellent hunter."

Her sudden wry grin distracted him and he nearly sliced off his thumb. "He was going to the Seminary near Alexandria before the war."

"Why did he fight for the South?"

Words unformed and thick stuck in his throat like mud.

"Did you have slaves?" she asked.

"No," he coughed. "No, but Gavin feared a too-strong federal government would destroy state's rights to govern themselves."

"And why did you fight?"

"Because everyone else was?" He tried to make a joke but she didn't laugh. He stared out over the clearing, the black patch in the center. "The history of our country should not be written in the blood of slaves. It is an abomination."

"Without slaves there will be no cotton," she said.

"Then there will be no cotton. It won't be the end of this country."

"It may be the end of the South," she said and he could not argue. "You don't speak of the war," she whispered. "You and Steven."

"It makes for terrible conversation." For a moment the only sound was the scrape of their knives through the rabbits. It was bloody work and she sat shoulder to shoulder with him. "Mostly it was just marching. So much marching."

"You weren't in many battles?"

"Plenty." There'd been a time he'd tried to memorize all of them. Fredericksburg, the Mud March, Chancellorsville, Gettysburg. After the Battle of the Wilderness and the fire . . . he stopped counting. He just kept marching. Loading his rifle, firing at the men he was supposed to kill, burning fields, destroying railroad tracks—and always, always marching.

"Were you injured? Ever?"

He shook his head, wishing he could understand why. He turned to find her gaping at him. "You are so . . . " *Damned*, he thought she might say. Or maybe she'd curse him because those fields he'd burned might have been hers, those men he killed might have been kin. "Lucky," she said.

His head pounded, his hands shook. "Is that what you call it?" he asked, taking his gun and leaving her surrounded by what he'd killed.

"Are you hunting again?"

He nodded, staring out at the forest, anywhere but at her.

"Take me with you," she said.

"You want to hunt?"

"I should learn."

"You're a fine shot." He remembered those three bullets in her husband.

"But a terrible tracker."

"You plan on tracking in Denver?"

"I plan on learning everything I can to survive."

He wanted to deny her, reject her company, but she already had the rabbits inside for her sister to string up for the smokehouse and her hands washed, and she was back on the porch with Jimmy's rifle before the words were formed in his mouth.

And then she was with him, beside him, her arm brushing his, making the nerves there sizzle awake. He'd thought in all his years marching through war that he'd seen all sides of pain. But the pain she wrought was new.

"I am sorry I let you go into the cabin with him that night," Cole said. "I knew . . . I knew he was going to hurt you."

"You tried to stop me."

He shook his head, unable to let her believe that. "No, I didn't. If I hadn't wanted you to go in there, you wouldn't have gone in. But I wanted whatever information he had about my brother. And that you got hurt —"

He couldn't look at her, this beautiful woman, who'd had means and background. She'd probably gone to church every Sunday, just like him. Perhaps she'd had dreams of family, of children and legacy. Her soul had at one time been as clean and pure as his.

And he'd handed her a gun. How did he fail to make the effort to save her soul from this terrible blackness in his? Why did he damn her this way?

"Are you angry?" he asked.

"About what?"

"About what I made you, handing you that gun?" He stared at the grass at her feet, the worn toe of her boot. She would need new ones before next winter.

A killer. I made you a killer.

"I'm grateful."

He flinched away from her words.

She stepped closer until he was suddenly looking into her eyes. They were blue, the color of the sky at home over the orchard at twilight. They would absolve him of his sins, those eyes, should he allow it.

"I'm grateful," she said again. "That's all you made me."

He turned away, gun in hand, to kill more things.

CHAPTER 8

AT DINNER STEVEN pulled out a crock of honey, golden and perfect. Melody clapped like it was Christmas morning.

"You've been keeping secrets," she cried.

"I forgot about it," Steven said. He did not smile, but his eyes were bright. An improvement over what he'd shown before.

"It has been a long time since we've had honey," she said, burning her fingers on the hot biscuits because she simply couldn't wait.

Annie did the same, the heat from the biscuits steaming her glasses, and she giggled. Actually giggled, and then as if she'd burped at the table, she clapped a hand over her mouth.

The sight of her sister so delighted made Melody giggle, too—the sound awkward and foreign like a duck barking, which made Annie drop her hand and laugh, and soon they were both wiping their eyes, holding their stomachs, in a true fit of gaiety. Like one of a million they'd had as girls, laughing so hard and so long they forgot what was so funny in the first place.

"Ladies," Cole said, his dark, rich voice cutting through their laughter, "the honey."

Shrieking, they used their fingers to wipe the table where the honey had dripped down from the biscuits. And then they licked their fingers.

It was decadent and girlish at the same time. And she had another strange flash of happiness. A sense that given sunlight and food and staying in the same place for a time, they would recover from all their wounds.

The happiness, so rare, made her giddy. Light.

A feeling she hadn't had in years.

And then she noticed Cole, sitting in the doorway, his plate on his knee, watching her with narrowed eyes.

Awareness sizzled up her spine.

Slowly, breathlessly aware of his eyes on her, she slipped her thumb from her mouth.

Cole's hands were slack around his plate. His gaze so warm against her skin, she felt as if she were too close to the fire.

"Would you like some?" she asked, tipping the honey crock toward him.

"No. Thank you."

His voice was like a touch of a hand across the nape of her neck, and it had been a long year, a long awful year since that had felt anything but terrifying.

In one horrible swollen moment, she was taken back to the easy ripe days when touches felt *good*.

Those stolen kisses, the frenzied caresses, the heated whispered words with Christopher, the scandalous behavior that brought all of it on—she'd liked it. All of it.

She'd gone to her wedding night with Jimmy a very experienced virgin. She doubted she was the only girl sending her fiancé off to war with more than just a goodbye kiss. So she knew that what Jimmy had done was not . . . not the only way it could be done. Pain was not the only result when a man and woman came together. There had been pleasure with Christopher.

And Cole's attention created an echo of that pleasure now.

Faint and dim, but a ripple under her skin nonetheless.

"Get my saddlebags, would you?" Steven asked, and Cole grabbed the leather bags from the pegs by the door.

"I just remembered I picked these up at the post office last time I was in Denver," Steven said, pulling the two books from his saddlebags. He handed Annie the book of poetry, which caused Melody's bookworm sister to nearly fall over herself with excitement.

"You like to read?" Steven asked. Annie nodded so hard her glasses slipped down her nose. "You're like Cole, then. There was never a book he didn't love."

"This one might be the first," Cole said, holding up the second pamphlet. "*Water Drilling Techniques in Oil Prospecting?*"

"If we're to be oil men, we'd better learn to do more than just gather it from seeps." Steven dug further into the bags. "This is for you."

He handed Cole a box, inside of which was a harmonica. In Cole's hand it glimmered in the firelight.

"You learned to play?" Cole asked. He stared at the instrument as if it was an old friend he thought he'd never see again.

"No." Steven shook his head. He was still pale, but he'd been sitting up for dinner. "I was going to teach myself. Or, in my better dreams, it was a gift for you when you arrived."

"You play?" Melody asked, and Cole nodded. He wore no hat and his sleeves were rolled up; he'd been taking down trees in the forest and sawing them into logs. Sawdust clung to the fine hair on his arms and the sunlight caught it and made him look like he'd been rolled in gold dust.

He held the silvery harmonica like a lover. The way Christopher used to hold her. And in a sudden spasm her body *remembered*. The echo of pleasure became a cacophony. Her skin remembered kindness and passion. Her breasts, between her legs, she remembered what being touched and stroked and held so gently felt like. The memory was like a hard rain on parched soil.

She put a hand to her chest, suddenly overcome.

"Play for us," Annie urged, and Cole lifted the harmonica to his lips.

There were starts and stops, a bad note that made them all cringe.

"It's been a while," he laughed, embarrassed.

"It sounds good no matter what," Melody whispered.

When he started to play in earnest, his music was beauty and torture. It was laughter and tears. Everything she felt, every sad and wonderful and lonely and happy feeling was turned to bittersweet music.

She and Annie asked for more. Another one. Still another. He ran out of songs to play and began to repeat them.

Cole watched her and she let him. She just let that music pry her right open, unable to stop it, as if her ribs were a clamshell. She could listen all—

"Stop," Steven whispered, and the music halted mid-note.

"Steven?" Cole stood up.

"No more, Cole," Steven whispered and he rolled over on his bed, his back to them. "Please don't play anymore."

COLE DIDN'T FALL asleep that night. The night of the harmonica and the honey. And the women laughing.

Usually he could fall into a fitful sleep for a few hours before the nightmares woke him up, but tonight he couldn't even get that far.

Instead, when the cabin was quiet he headed out to the barn where he lit a lamp and measured and sawed logs for the addition to the barn.

Melody's horses softly nickered in welcome and reached out their noses for a pat. The horses were fine company for an insomniac.

He had not slept more than five hours a night in six years. And it was worse here.

The ghosts would not let him rest. Like moths attracted to a flame, they swarmed under the moonlight. And tonight he was doubly plagued.

Melody, her thumb in her mouth, her eyes on him. He'd been destroyed in that glance.

For days now he'd ignored his body's response to her, because she'd been so hurt. Because he owed her so much, because he'd thought it had been burned out of him. Softness, want. *Desire.* He had not thought of a woman like that in . . . years. He did not partake of the whores or the grateful widows, the desperate girls along his route to Colorado. If he was able, he would flip them some coins and try not to look in their eyes.

There had been a woman in St. Louis he'd spent dark, desperate nights with, but one morning he woke up and she was gone with his horse and all of his money.

But tonight. That honey . . . He imagined taking Melody's hand, sucking that finger into his own mouth.

And then when he'd sucked off every last lingering taste on her fingers, he would lift that honey crock and pour it across her lips, down her neck. He'd cover her breasts with it. Trail it across her belly. He imagined her sucking his flesh the way she'd sucked her own, with her eyes closed, the purr of satisfaction in her throat.

Christ. Stop.

His hands shaking, his blood burning through his veins, he picked up Steven's saw and went to work, hoping that with enough effort he might be able to roll the stone back in front of his cave, eliminating the light that made it so hard to see.

Her laughter made him feel shackled. It teased him with hope of an entirely different kind of freedom.

Hours later the lamp burned out and sunlight came through the cracks near the goat's head.

Coffee. It was time for coffee.

Stepping out into the clearing, he saw Annie and Melody

standing over a tree stump with an open leather satchel.

They were a pretty sight, pretty enough to make him pause.

Melody made him pause.

She wore no bonnet and her hair was swept up into a tight knot of gold at the back of her head. The sight of her neck, the knobs of her spine pressing against her tender white skin, made his blood pound.

His hands twitched as if they had the ability to remember the feel of her waist when he'd helped her out of the flowers. The nimble strength of her, the taut nature of her skin and muscle.

He'd succeeded last night and pushed the memory of the honey and her fingers and the laughter in her eyes entirely out of his brain. It no longer existed. It never happened.

Except seeing her now, like this at dawn, the memory exploded in him like cannon fire and his defenses were destroyed.

"Cole?" Melody said, catching sight of him as he came into the clearing. "You are up early."

I cannot sleep because of you. Because of guilt. And want. And because after all that has happened you are able to giggle over honey and lie down in flowers, smile up at a blue sky as if your soul is undamaged.

I cannot sleep for envy.

For wanting you.

"I could say the same. What are you two up to?"

"Our seeds and plants," she said. "We're seeing what's still alive."

He stepped forward, intrigued.

"The roses are dead," Melody said.

"They're just sleeping," Cole said. "You can wake them up."

"You're a gardener and a musician?" Melody asked.

And a soldier and murderer...I'm all of these things at the same time and it is tearing me apart.

"We owned an orchard. A large one. I used to know

something about making things grow."

"Used to?" she teased.

His skin grew hot under his collar. Melody's eyes, surrounded by that yellowing bruise, looked right into him. Right through him.

When he'd crossed the Mississippi, he'd gotten sick in the waves, and his stomach had rushed to his brains and then sunk down to his feet. Only to return, unable to make up its mind. This feeling he got when she looked at him was similar.

Perhaps because he was so unsure of what she was seeing. How ridiculous it would be to ask, *When you look at me, what do you see?*

"Cole?" Annie asked, diverting his attention. "What do you recommend we do with the roses?"

Right. Roses.

He glanced back down at the tangled root. One was drier than the other; it might not survive planting, but he had seen worse.

"You need to plant them," he said. "You won't be able to keep them alive like that much longer."

Annie and Melody shared a sad look before Melody said, "Then you will have something to remember us by, come summer. They were our mother's joy."

Oh, Christ, why did that make him feel like weeping? He had not wept since word had reached him that Lee had surrendered. But since being in this clearing he'd felt the burn of tears with surprising regularity.

"We will be honored," he told them.

"Not if they're dead," Melody said.

"The key," he said with a sudden smile, "is manure. And lots of water."

"Finally, we are lucky in our horse shit," Melody muttered, dry as a bone.

Annie smacked her sister's arm but he laughed. And between the lack of laughter in his life and her surprising sense of humor, he was helpless and he laughed until tears formed in his eyes.

"Pick out a place," he said and went into the barn for his own broad shovel and Steven's smaller spade, and then he went around to the far side of the barn, near the rocky outcropping where Steven had started the manure pile.

He scooped up a shovelful and took it out to the women, who had selected spots on either side of the rough porch, near the stone foundation.

"Good choice," he said.

"We thought in the summer it would smell good," Melody said. "As well as be beautiful."

"I think you're right." With the spade he dug two holes in the turned earth and mixed in the manure. He poured half a bucket of water into each of the holes and waited while Annie and Melody unwrapped all of the burlap that they'd obviously tried to keep damp as they traveled and placed the root balls into the holes.

He covered them up with soil and manure and put more water over them. From the earth came the dark, loamy scent of his childhood and it set loose a hundred memories of walking the orchard with his father. Duke, his dog, at his side.

There were more. Thousands more. Countless.

The drone of bees feasting on the rotting fallen apples, the way they buzzed drunk against his face and hands.

The smell of the flowers at first bloom and Father taking some to tuck in Mother's steel-gray hair.

The shoulder-breaking work of harvest, Steven complaining all the while.

Samantha with the water bucket and dipper, trying to be a part of the work. Angry when mother kept her away.

"There," Melody said, coming to her feet. "Thank you very much—"

"What else is in that bag?" he asked. "Your seeds."

"Beans, corn, strawberries, tomatoes, pumpkins—"

"I'll buy them."

Melody blinked at him and he supposed he was being slightly alarming. But he was suddenly thinking of Father, and Duke the dog, and the smell of the fog burning off the fields in the morning. And he realized in a terrible, awful rush that the dream he'd thought was dead still had life.

These memories had broken down the doors he tried to keep them behind.

He wanted something to grow and care for and leave behind for the future. And he wanted it ferociously, like a starving man in front of a plate of food.

Hope had returned to him. Because what was planting but the very embodiment of hope? Of faith. Of belief. A shiver ran over his body.

"Not all of them—you will want to have some for your own home. But I will buy some."

"How many of the seeds do you want?"

"Five dollars' worth—"

"For seeds?" Melody laughed.

For your future, he thought. *For mine. Is that the price of a soul? Because I'll pay whatever you want for the damn seeds.*

She looked over his head toward the mountains behind him for a long time and he wondered what she was thinking. What were the scales in her head and how did they work?

"How do I even know you have all this money you've promised us?" she asked.

"You don't believe me?"

"It is not personal." She tugged down her sleeves, as if she were merchant behind her counter. It was . . . attractive, the way she fought for herself. "But I would like this money in advance."

He nodded, admiring her.

Inside the house, he pulled out his saddlebags and handed her five silver one-dollar coins. It took some effort to pretend he didn't see her hands shaking as she tucked them into her own bags, but he wanted to give her the privacy of her pride.

They negotiated over the seeds for most of the morning. Annie grew tired of it and left to check on Steven, leaving Melody and Cole to haggle over the tree stump.

"I don't know that the pumpkins will grow in this soil," she said.

"I would still like to try."

"Seems a waste to sell you a seed we both know won't grow."

A strand of hair fell across her cheek and he wanted to brush it back.

"Have a little faith," he whispered.

She shot him an arch look and then looked quickly back down at the seeds. "That, I'm afraid, is a rarer commodity than your brother's oil."

"Your family were not farmers?"

"My family might have been, I certainly wasn't. We had cotton and hay, but Father was a doctor and we raised horses. We had a kitchen garden, but until the war the slaves took care of it. When they left, we did what we could."

He made a low sound in his throat. "Farming is faith and foresight. And luck." *And hope. So much goddamned hope*, he thought, sorting through the bean seeds, removing the cracked ones that would not grow. It all came back to him, the routines and rituals. His father had not just been a farmer; he'd been a steward of the land. A caretaker. And he'd passed that on to Cole. "It is faith in the soil, in the weather, in the seed."

"I would not make a good farmer," she said, and their eyes caught and he felt a lightning strike of lust. The color on her cheeks indicated she was not immune to it either. "I'm decidedly out of faith."

"You were the woman who lay down in flowers."

"The head injury, remember?"

He smiled at her gruff efforts at self-preservation because he understood them so well.

"You can do your part," he said, and took one of the linen strips that she and Annie had used to bandage Steven and spread it out over a stump. "Prepare the soil. The seed. It feels less like chance when you do that."

He placed his seeds there, separated into the different fruits and vegetables, and then folded the linen over it before pouring water over the whole thing.

"What are you doing?" she asked.

"Preparing the seeds," he said. "Getting them ready." *Trying to rebuild my faith. Perhaps yours, too. If you can lie down in flowers, weep at harmonica music, laugh over honey...then maybe I can hope again.*

"I won't be here," she said. "To see any of this bloom."

Some inner voice whispered that wasn't true, but he did not know how to listen to it.

"You will have a garden in Denver," he said.

"We don't have enough money for a tent, much less a house with a garden." She laughed, but he could see the worry she was trying so hard to banish staining the edges of her smile.

"Do you think we won't help?" he asked, catching her eye. "We will get you a house. Plant you a garden."

It was a promise, and after a long moment she nodded as if she understood.

"What happens next?" she asked.

And Cole, breathing deep, breathing all the way down into the crippled and withered edges of his lungs for the first time in years, answered, "We wait."

FOR THE REST of the week they waited. Cole checked his seeds every day, and every day Melody pretended not to be interested, claiming her faith was all gone, but he could see her curiosity for what it was.

"Today?" she asked.

"Not today," he said.

ENOUGH TIME PASSED and the skin on many of the seeds

had lost their wrinkles. The seeds themselves had swollen and split, revealing the tender white flesh of a sprout.

"Today," he said when he caught her eye. "But first I'm going to prepare the soil."

He went outside and after a while she followed, with a full rag bag and the beginnings of a rug.

He brought the manure by the shovelful and dumped it over the dirt. He could no longer pretend not to be aware of what was happening to him in this clearing. Day after day, moment by moment, he was finding the man he'd been— battered, bruised, different in so many ways, but underneath the blood and the dirt, he was still recognizable to himself.

He was painfully aware of her watching him, waiting on the edges as if she didn't know what to do. He could feel her there; her desire to work with him was palpable. Exciting.

Yes, he thought. *Do this with me.*

"I could help you," Melody said, having abandoned the rug and picked up the spade he'd left on the stump. "If you like."

He nodded, thrilled to his core. "Thank you."

She used the spade to mix the manure into the dirt. It was dirty, sweaty work and she did not complain or stop. He handed her his gloves.

"I'm fine," she said, probably by rote. But he took her bare hand in his, and the softness of it, the *foreignness* of it was like putting his hand in fire. He turned her wrist and touched each of the fingers she held in a fist. One by one, like the petals of a flower at dawn, they opened and revealed the red, raw spots on her palm.

"Please," he said. His breath moved the hair at her temple, and he wondered how long it had been since he'd been so close to a lady. She smelled of dirt and sweat, and lavender of all things. He wanted to close his eyes and press his nose to her temple, where the sweat of her skin had run into her hair. He wanted to kiss the pale pink of her cheeks, the soft skin behind her ear. The heartbeat that pounded in her neck. He could see it. He actually lifted his hand to touch it before he stopped himself.

"Wear the gloves," he said and stepped away.

She was beautiful and desirable and strong. He could not keep up with all the ways she was surprising him.

A few hours later, they took a break for water and side meat shoved inside split leftover biscuits. "You are a hard worker," Cole said, resting his hands on the edge of his spade. Melody blew a long strand of blonde hair out of her face before sending him a wry look.

"Not always." She took a piece of bacon out of the sandwich to eat separately. "I was the hottest of the hothouse flowers. As spoiled as they come."

"Seems unlikely from where I sit."

"Trust me, I . . . wasn't very nice."

"I'm not sure you are now." He winked at her when she looked up at him, ready to be angry.

"And I suppose you used to be funny?" The teasing between them was potent, like his mother's brandy cherries. His skin prickled with awareness, not just of her, but of himself. Of what he was doing, this careful and cautious easing out of himself. Like a hermit crab walking away from his shell.

"I used to be lighter," he told her, spinning the shovel under his hands, just so he had something to do. "Easier, I think." She was looking at him and so he resolutely did not look at her. "My brother would say I was always serious, but it wasn't always so difficult to be—" *with people. In my own skin.* He stopped, unsure of what he was about to say, much less how to say it.

"I've never been able to understand how Annie was able to be so happy," she said as if she knew what had been in his head. Those thoughts he'd been unable to really make sense of. Not just that she knew, but that she understood. He'd been about to say *happy.* He used to be solemn and serious and slow to joke, but he'd been *happy.*

"Even before the war," Melody continued. "Lined up against the wall at parties, avoiding the eyes of every man in attendance, it didn't seem to matter to her. I never understood how, when we were alone, she could laugh, she could make me laugh. She found purpose and happiness in the strangest places. Well, strange to me at the time, since I was fully invested in those parties. My worth was tied directly to my dance card. I admired that about her, how she determined her own way. Refused to be cowed when she didn't have to be. And during the war I admired her even more. She would not let herself lose faith. Or heart. She still somehow made me laugh." Melody's sky-blue eyes clouded over, and he knew she had a darkness, too. Inside, perhaps, where other people had happiness, or joy, or fond memories of the person they'd been—the two of them had darkness.

"Why did Jimmy call her mute?"

"When she was younger she was painfully shy. She had a stammer that was only made worse in company."

"She doesn't have a stammer now."

"No. She outgrew it for the most part. Though she was still shy. Until the war, actually. Helping father, I guess, gave her confidence. But when I married Jimmy, he remembered her from before the war. He mocked her stammer, and I think . . . I think she chose not to talk to him. She let him believe whatever he wanted."

"That must have been difficult."

"I don't think it was for her. She never cared what he thought of her. What anyone thought of her. You should know, before you think to pity her, I was tempted to let your brother die. I knew what would happen if Jimmy found out that we had saved him and I wasn't sure a stranger was worth . . . that. My sister, however, was undeterred."

"I do not pity either of you."

The stiff way she held her shoulders told him all too well that she didn't believe him. She found herself pitiful.

"I wish you could see yourself as I see you," he said. The words were so startling she looked up at him, her eyes wide. Her mouth agape.

Quickly, embarrassed, he bent his head back to his work.

A fool, drunk on hope.

CHAPTER 9

THAT NIGHT IT was fish again, fried in bacon fat with some of the onions from behind the barn, and the last of the biscuits.

"A feast!" Cole proclaimed, pulling up the stump he usually sat on.

"You are easy to please," Melody said, still not quite able to look him in the eye.

I wish you could see yourself as I see you.

The words would not stop rolling through her. A tide gone mad. She wanted to grab onto the implication of those words, that he saw her as something special. Something different, perhaps more than she was. And she wanted to be that person. Clear and clean of all she'd done, bright in his eyes.

"It's not beans and it's not hardtack. I am happy."

And he was, everyone could see that. Something had happened to him over the last weeks, as he'd planted those seeds, and there was a lightness in him where there hadn't been before. And it was so . . . pleasing to see. So satisfying.

But at the same time it made her wary. It made her want to cry out a warning.

Be careful of your joy. It will not last.

Happiness didn't come without a cost and the cost was always too high.

And it made her realize her own happiness the last two weeks was not yet paid for. She'd been unguarded and perhaps foolish.

The fire behind them was warm and crackling and the cabin was full of good smells and enough food for all of them. And it was rare enough that they all seemed to take note. They all seemed aware of how lean their souls had become.

Her sister, lovely and serious, was alight in the fire's warmth. And Melody tried to force herself not to worry about the cost of such moments. But she could feel the spectre of repayment in the shadows of the cabin.

These moments do not come free.

"My brother says you intend to stay in Denver," Steven said as they all tucked into their fish. Piercing the crispy silvery skin and letting out all the steam.

"We do," Annie said, "once you are well enough to take us."

"And dig our garden," Melody added, catching Cole's eye.

"Do you understand what Denver is?" Steven asked, and Melody and Annie shared startled looks. Steven was not asking casually. He seemed angry. Affronted by their plans to go.

"Steven," Cole murmured, "this is not our business."

Steven turned on his brother as best he could with his bandages still tight around his belly. "You would send them to Denver alone?"

"We will give them enough money—"

"Money!" Steven cried. "So they can buy an opium den? Or better yet a saloon?"

"No, a home. Steven, what has gotten into you? It's a start. Melody is a widow and Denver is full of widows."

Steven gaped at him as if Cole had suggested they saddle Melody and Annie like horses. "You know what happens to widows when the money runs out."

Whore houses. That was the work Steven referred to. Melody felt herself grow cold at the mention of what no one talked about. That was what awaited women who were not careful. Who did not secure their futures.

"There are women who do honest work there. Seamstresses, laundry, the hotel—" Cole said.

"Would you want our sister working herself to the bone at a laundry?" Steven asked.

"They are not our sisters. They are free to make up their own minds."

"No. They are not. But they are undoubtedly someone's sisters. A soldier, perhaps a boy one of us killed."

Annie's fork dropped from her hand and she pressed her fingers to her lips.

"Forgive my brother," Cole said, his dark eyes glittering in the firelight. "He forgets himself."

No, thought Melody, a strange fury building in her chest. A terrible desire to rattle all the chains that bound her. *It was me that forgot. That allowed myself to get swept up in my sister's talk of freedom. In the strange peace of this place that was never going to be mine. The world outside of this clearing is a cruel one for women and I had let myself forget.*

"I worked with my father in field hospitals during the war," said Annie, once she had recovered herself. The rim of her glasses reflected gold in the ever-darkening room. "There are doctors in Denver, and doctors are always in need of competent assistants. We have three horses that will fetch a handsome price. And as you have said, you intend to pay us. We are far from destitute."

"You don't want a family? A husband?"

"I want to be of use," Annie said. Melody wondered what Annie meant by that. Was being a wife and mother not of use? While Melody held no illusions about the role of wife, the dream of mother still held beauty and purpose to her. That stubborn dream of home and family still clung to her.

"And you, Melody?" Steven asked, shaking Melody from her thoughts. "What will you do?"

"You mean until I am to be a whore?" she asked. It was satisfying when everyone reacted with shock. What was the point of being shocking if no one reacted? "I think I will strap on guns," she said, looking at Cole. "And if you are to be a farmer, I will take your place as a killer."

Sap popped in the fire, the only sound in the room besides the harsh saw of Annie's breathing.

"I have lost my appetite," Melody said into the stillness, and stood. "I am for bed."

Privacy was a sham in this cottage and in the darkness of the bedroom, her hands in fists pressed to her lips, Melody heard Annie say, "Excuse her. I fear the last few weeks have taken a toll on my sister."

A toll, yes. Quite. A goddamned toll.

"It's the war," Steven muttered. "It's ruined all of us. Cole, help me to bed."

Melody lay down on her bedroll and imagined her lovely supper going to waste and wished Steven was wrong.

ROLLING OFF THE bedroll the next morning was not as painful as it had been. Melody's muscles ached from the work she'd been doing, but she felt her body getting stronger. The bones always so visible beneath her skin were slowly being buried by flesh from the plentiful food.

Her bruises from Jimmy's fist were fading.

She'd let her lack of fear make her complacent, that much was clear after last night. She'd been lulled by this safety she felt, this contentment, into believing that they would be all right. That they had survived the worst the world could offer them.

But Steven had reminded her there were more horrors out there.

She changed into her cleanest dress, Mother's bombazine.

Before heading west, Melody and Annie had spent days tailoring their dresses to fit without crinolines, but still the skirts on this old mourning gown dragged.

And halfway through the war she and Annie had given up on corsets, having lost so much weight as to make them ridiculous.

So, the gloomy black dress fell like a sack around her body.

To seduce Christopher she'd had new gowns from Atlanta, and Maisey's milk baths twice a week. Rose water she and Annie had made themselves. Now she had a black eye, turning yellow, and a tattered, second-hand mourning gown.

And she decidedly did not smell of roses.

The thought was very nearly funny.

Why am I thinking of Christopher? she wondered. Though she knew. In her heart she knew. The decision was being made deep in her belly where all her fears lived.

"Where are the men?" Melody asked, stepping into the main room of the cabin. Wincing, she attempted to pull up her hair.

"Cole wanted to share his plans for building a corral, and Steven felt up for the exercise." Annie wiped her hands on her apron. "Let me."

Melody sat on a stool and allowed her sister to fuss over her. It was familiar and lovely, her sister's deft fingers combing through her hair.

"I am sorry about last night," Melody said. "I'm afraid I don't know what got into me."

"You have been through so much."

"I think we all have. All of us in this cabin." It had felt last night like the pain all of them carried was pushing against the logs, attempting to lift the roof as if that was the only way the ghosts could get free.

"All the more reason for us to be shut of this place."

Melody sighed with pleasure at her sister's touch. The tabletop was cluttered with bottles and bits of linen. Surgical tools and pieces of buckskin pierced with needles. Annie had been going through Father's bag and sorting out the empty bottles. Melody picked up a blue bottle, twirling it in the sunlight streaming through the door.

Pretty, but empty.

"Do you really not want children?" Melody asked, wincing when Annie's brush hit a tangle.

"Mother made it very clear that my leg and my shyness would not win me a husband. Children were never going to be for me."

"But you have much to offer a man—"

Annie put down the brush with a clatter. "Is this a joke?"

"No . . . I think Steven—"

"Do you think after watching what you suffered in the name of marriage that I would raise my hand to be next?"

"Not all marriages were like mine. Our parents—"

"Stop, Melody. We are going to Denver. We will make our own way."

Once, when they were kids, Annie convinced herself that they had a baby brother who had been lost. She convinced Melody too, Melody who believed everything her older sister said, who would follow her sister into fire if Annie had suggested it. And they'd spent the summer searching the property for that baby. Mama finally put a stop to it when their brother found Annie and Melody trying to get a boat into the river behind the house.

Your sister has different ideas, Mama had said. *And they can be dangerous; you have to have more sense. Keep her safe from following these ideas of hers.*

In every city they traveled through, the soul-dead eyes of whores and laundry girls, of widows with dirty hungry children pulling at their skirts, watched them from the balconies and doorways of saloons and shacks.

A warning for women to trust wisely. To take care.

Did those women think they would make their own way?

Were they now paying the price for past happiness?

"I seduced Christopher into marriage," she said, apropos of nothing. "Did you know that?"

"The town of Savannah knew that."

Christopher had been engaged to Rebecca Townsley, and because Melody had wanted Christopher, because she liked the future she imagined with him on his family's grand plantation, she stole him away like a trinket she was fond of. At the beginning of October, on her birthday, Melody had batted her eyelashes, danced too close. On Thanksgiving she kissed him in a dark corner. Allowed him shocking liberties at Christmas, and then orchestrated her father walking in on them at the New Year's party.

Seducing a man into marriage had been surprisingly easy. Christopher had been a simple man, really. And as a girl she'd thought they could make each other happy by just being young and pretty and wealthy. Older now, with a terrible marriage behind her, she knew they would not have been happy. They would have been hateful within a few years. Bitter and sighing. She imagined the girl she'd been growing up to be the kind of woman who threw things.

She did not dream in colors as vibrant as happiness for her future. But contentment did not seem out of the question. And contentment only required reason.

And bravery.

"We are not the girls we were," Annie said. "And this is not Savannah."

"No, it's not." Melody laughed, wondering how her sister did not see the danger. "It's far more dangerous."

"We will be fine," Annie said. "As long as we're together, we will be fine."

What if those words don't work anymore?

And in the face of what Annie was proposing, they were ludicrous. Like trying to keep out a hurricane with greased paper. She could laugh at Annie's idea of the two of them safe and allowed to do what they liked. Perhaps at one time she would have been cruel enough to do that. To kill this dream in her sister's lovely brown eyes. But today she could not do it. She would let her sister have her dream.

And she would set out for a husband.

HONESTLY, NEVER HAD she imagined that getting herself married again would require so much dirt. But the world was a different place, and if she meant to stay in this clearing and secure her future, and that of her sister, it meant seducing Cole.

And Cole farmed.

As they worked side by side in the garden, she had to put away all her sympathy for him. All her curiosity. She was going to manipulate him and she found she could not think of his will. Those nightmares that kept him working all night. The darkness behind his eyes. The way he'd grabbed on to planting this garden as if it were a rope he could use to climb out of hell.

She had to view him as she'd once viewed Christopher, a prize to be won.

This too was who she'd been before the war.

After they'd planted the seeds that were ready, Cole carefully folded up the linen, carrying it inside as if it were a babe in danger of catching a chill. She sat down on one of the stumps and let her muscles and bones slump. Mama wasn't here to tell her to sit up.

Mama wasn't here to see anything. And for that Melody was grateful. She'd shocked Mama plenty, but what she was planning now would have sent her into hysterics.

Cole came back out, rolling down his shirt sleeves, as the sun had set behind the western pines and the cold was settling in. She barely noticed.

"Your sister has made more biscuits, and my brother is talking of an afternoon walk to the seeps. It seems we've all been busy."

"I had to marry Jimmy," she said, because there was no way to ease into the conversation. She stared down at her hands in the gloves that he'd insisted she wear. "I thought I did, anyway."

He stopped and she could tell by his tension, his stillness, that he was listening with his whole body. Such attention was disarming, but flattering too. She'd never been so *important* to a man. Not Christopher. Certainly not Jimmy. Not even her father.

Annie might have had that joy, but to her father, Melody was simply frivolous.

This marriage would not be a hardship with a man who paid such attention to her.

"I . . . I don't judge you. We've all had to do things we probably wished we hadn't."

"He was my fiancé's brother. Christopher died . . . so many good men died, and Jimmy came back." She nearly laughed, though none of it was funny. Jimmy's survival seemed proof that God had not been watching those battlefields. "Father was dead, my brother too. Mama. And our slaves—" She forced herself to look right at him, this man who went to war, who risked his life for something she hadn't thought twice about until forced to. Add that to the pile of things he could judge her for. "Our slaves were gone and Annie and me... we did the best we could, but it was just the two of us and so much work. Jimmy offered marriage and I agreed, but he didn't do the work, either, and there was no money and no one would work for him."

"You didn't know his nature before the war?"

"He was . . . changed. He drank too much. His temper was tenuous."

"Why are you telling me this?"

"I have to look after my sister. And I thought all the decisions I was making would do that."

He walked toward her and she realized how tall he was. How serious. In her life before she wouldn't have picked him even to dance; she liked men who smiled. And knew how to flirt and play her games. This man didn't know how to flirt. You could tell by looking at him, the stone and steel of him was not made for such a thing. He might have been easier before the war, but he was never fun.

She'd liked fun.

Now, she liked the way he cared for those seeds. The way he looked at her as he crossed the field. His face in the firelight—she liked that, too. The way he played the harmonica and laughed when she said shocking things.

"Your sister seems set on Denver."

"I think my sister has a false idea of what our lives would be like there."

"Do . . . do you have no other family? No one else to go to?"

She shook her head.

"My brother," he said, "thought to sell a barrel of oil from the seeps and give the money to you. He said that would be enough to get you passage on a wagon train heading back to St. Joseph. From there you can get the train and head east."

"There's nothing back east for us."

"Then you could go west."

"And try our luck with the Indians?"

He glanced away. "Tell me what you would have us do, Melody?"

You know, she thought. *Don't make me do this. Please. You know.*

But in the end he was silent and she had no choice.

"Marry me."

CHAPTER 10

COLE STEPPED BACK, stunned, but not by her boldness. No, he was shocked by his own reaction. A recoil of the soul.

Not at her, but what she was proposing.

"It . . . it makes good sense," she stammered when he was silent. "This land will prosper with all of us working."

"I can hire men for that," he stammered and she flinched, color draining from her skin.

"You can't hire men to have your children," she whispered.

No. But she was all but suggesting he hire her.

His parents' love had been a tangible cloud around them. They stole kisses on the porch, walked hand in hand to church. It never occurred to him that his own marriage would be anything less than that.

"You speak of this like it's a business arrangement—I offer you security and you offer me free labor and children?"

Her eyes blazed. "I am sorry I can no longer offer you my fine dowry or some of Father's acreage near the river."

"I don't want those things."

"Then what do you want?" she snapped.

He had thought the war and his two years as a hired gun had killed not only the expectation that he would marry, but that he would marry for love. And yet, here it was. Marriage would solve the problem of Melody and her sister. And he could not pretend that he didn't want her. He did. More every minute.

He could marry Melody to keep her and her sister safe.

He could marry her to atone for his sins.

But that wasn't the marriage he wanted.

As beautiful as she was, as interesting and strong—he wanted a marriage that wasn't born of desperation.

"More." The word slid out of him, a whisper, a breath. True despite its meager entrance into the world. He wanted more than her cold proposition.

"What more is there?" she nearly spat.

"You have just been freed from a terrible marriage. How can you be sure I am not as bad or worse than Jimmy?"

She lifted her chin. "You overpaid me for the seeds."

He laughed despite himself. "You're easy to convince."

"You are kind, you work hard, don't appear to drink."

"There isn't anything to drink."

"Still, you're of . . . pleasing face and form." That she blushed at those words sent blood pounding through his veins. Suddenly he wondered how long she'd been staring at him while he shaved before he'd pulled his shirt on. Apparently the answer was awhile.

"You are of pleasing face and form, as well," he murmured.

"I would be a good wife. I have been trained." Images of sex bloomed in his mind and he turned away, embarrassed by his thoughts. She was a woman who had been abused sorely by her husband, and thinking that way about her was to compound the injury done to her.

"I meant," she said, stammering and blushing as if she'd seen the thoughts in his head, "I can care for you. Children. For our home. Even out here."

She'd dragged Steven across a field to a cave; he had faith she could do anything she had to.

"Jimmy's brother, before the war, did you love him?" he asked.

"No." She laughed as if the idea was outrageous. "I loved the future he would bring me. The status. Father approved of our lands being joined. Thinking about it, I'm not sure that I thought enough about him to even like him. I could not tell you what his favorite season was, or food. I don't remember the color of his eyes. What he dreamt of. What he wanted. But I went to great lengths to make sure that he loved me. That . . . I would have the life I wanted."

Her honesty was astounding. He wasn't sure he'd ever met a person more ready to face who they'd been. It was brave. It made him like her more.

But he was not Christopher and he would not have her think he was.

"I was in love with a girl from the neighboring farm," he told her. "Jane. We were engaged practically since birth."

She snapped her mouth shut so hard her teeth clicked. "Is . . . do you still love her?"

"No. After the war, I couldn't stay in West Virginia. I had to find my brother. And she looked at me and . . . expected the old me, I think. I wasn't that person anymore. It was a relief to leave her. And I think she was relieved. "

"So, you are free."

Free. Yes, he was. Though not in the way she thought. He was free from that cave. His chains destroyed by her laughter and seeds. The hope she'd returned to him.

He would have her free in the same manner.

He was close enough that he could see the dirt caught in the sweat of her neck. Gnats buzzed around her hair, which was golden and wild in the sunlight.

"Do you truly want to be married again?"

"I am a woman," she said. "It's what we do."

"If you had freedom—"

"My sister tried to play this game with me," she said.

"Freedom is an adventure. I have had enough of adventure. I want security. Home. Children. People to . . . "

"Love?"

"I am not that much a fool. Not anymore."

How astounding to realize that he was. He was that fool.

"But I would like to have someone to care for. Work beside." Tears stood out in her eyes and she blinked them away. Such power she had. Such control.

"What is the difference?" he asked.

"I don't know. But love, faith, trust . . . all those things bring ruin to women. And I have been ruined enough."

"None of us can ever get back what we lost," he whispered.

"I know," she said. "But it doesn't mean I have to live in exile from what I want for the rest of my life, does it?"

Her words shook him to his core and he realized that was what he'd been doing for long, long years.

Living in exile.

From the life he wanted.

And she would offer back to him a cold shadow of what he wanted. And they both deserved better than that.

CHAPTER 11

HE WAS GOING to refuse. It was obvious. Anxiety opened like a great hole under her feet and she realized that this was her moment to be brave.

She stood up from the tree stump, the bark catching at her skirts. She put a hand to her trembling belly and tried to sound . . . unafraid.

"I . . . I am not unwilling. If that's what you are worried about," she said, and he stared at her blankly. "Because of Jimmy."

Before he could say anything she stepped toward him, stopping only when she could feel his chest against hers. The tips of her breasts, every time she took a breath, touched him, and heat and fear rattled through her in equal measure.

He is not like Jimmy, she told herself.

"What are you doing, Melody?"

Being brave. Caring for my sister. Securing my future. Trying to resurrect the dream for the third time.

None of those were things she could say. There were, in fact, no words that would convey all the things she was doing.

So she kissed him.

He stood stock still against her and she wasn't entirely sure what to do next. With Christopher this was all that had been required. She would kiss him and he'd manage the rest.

And Jimmy . . . The thought of what he'd done swallowed her bravery and she nearly stepped back. Nearly ran.

This is the only way, she thought, and forced herself to stay there, even as she began to shake with tension.

Cole was as still as she was, those lips—really very soft—unmoving against hers.

She stepped closer, until their bellies touched, and she felt the contact simmer through her. Ignoring her fear, she reached up to twine her hands around his neck. She found the soft silk of his hair and the heat of his skin.

So hot, his skin was so hot. And his chest so hard against hers. He was a wall of strength and heat. He was bigger than Christopher and Jimmy.

Do not run, she told herself. *Do not.*

His hands wrapped around her waist, and the bite of his fingers into her skin through her dress made her jerk backwards, breaking the kiss. She leaned away from his grip on her waist and he dropped his hands.

"You're terrified," he whispered.

"I'm not, I'm—"

"You're terrified and you would still seduce me into marrying you?" he asked.

It was hard to believe she'd ever thought his dark eyes were cold. They burned her flesh and she wished she could turn away, run somewhere to hide, but there was nowhere.

She lifted her chin and answered his question with silence. But there were ashamed tears burning behind her eyes.

I am desperate. And you know that.

"You are shaking with fear," he whispered.

"It is desire."

His eyes called her a liar.

After a moment he stepped closer, and hope and fear made her heart hammer in her chest. His hands lifted and gathered hers in their warm, solid grip. But he did not kiss her, or shove himself against her. He just held her hands and looked into her eyes, as if she were a book he was trying to read.

It will be okay, she told herself. They would all be okay. He was kind and his lips were soft and perhaps . . . perhaps she had done enough and they could stay here. In this safe place.

Finger by finger he pulled the gloves off her, until he had them in one hand and her hands in the other. The rough scrape of his calloused thumb against the tender skin of her wrist made her twitch.

With his eyes on her, he did it again.

"Cole . . . "

And then again.

"What are you doing?"

Again. Every brush of his thumb there uncoiled her until the fourth time he did it, a gasp escaped. She dropped her eyes.

Say something, please, release me from this uncertainty.

He lifted his hand to her lips, his thumb touching the corner of her mouth, and she could barely breathe for the tension in her body. The pain and pleasure of his touch. Of this doubt.

"Does that hurt?" he asked.

"No," she breathed, and he touched her lip again, the weight of his thumb pulling it down until the damp interior was revealed.

"Are you scared?" he whispered.

She shook her head.

"You're lying. And you don't need to. You can always tell me the truth."

"Before," she whispered. "I was scared. I'm . . . I'm not now."

He was so gentle, so careful, that the fear slipped away, replaced by that echo of pleasure. Her skin burned where they touched, the fire spreading from her wrist, up her arm. Her eyes fluttered shut.

"I must say no to the type of marriage you are proposing," he said.

Her eyes snapped open. "What?"

"I want something more than desperation."

She slapped his hands away. "Are you talking about love?"

He was, and he couldn't believe it himself.

"What if it's not impossible?" he breathed.

"You don't think that." Her scorn was crushing, but he didn't wince away from it.

"I want to. I want to believe that I can feel something good in this life again. That the war has not killed everything. If I get married . . . I want it to be born in those things—happiness, hope. Love. Isn't that what you want?"

She should have said yes. She should have convinced him she was falling in love with him right now, this moment, but she couldn't. There were some lies even she could not speak.

"Even before the war I was not that kind of woman." Her engagement to Christopher was born in pride and greed and selfishness. In her will to control.

"Perhaps you are now."

"Now?" She laughed. "Now, I am barren inside."

"I thought I was too," he told her, and then glanced down at the garden. "But now, I am not so sure."

He was speaking in stupid childish riddles and she would have him be plain.

"What do you want from me?"

"More," he breathed. "I want more."

MELODY WALKED ON wobbly legs toward the cabin, away from Cole and his devastating touch. The front door was open and she heard her sister inside, the rattle of the rake as she smoothed the floor.

Unable to go inside and pretend that all was well, she collapsed on the edge of the porch, her hands clasped in the folds of her muddy skirt.

She'd proposed and been rejected.

The October she'd turned seventeen, eight years ago, when the war was just a rumbling in sitting rooms while the men smoked cigars, she'd been proposed to ten times. Ten times. But she'd held out for Christopher, campaigning for his hand with skill General Lee would have admired.

She pushed the back of her wrist into her forehead when the world spun.

There wasn't any *more* in her. Any love. She wasn't sure she'd ever had the capacity for that.

"I don't believe you," Annie said, and Melody stiffened. Annie must have seen her kissing Cole, and now she was here to lecture her.

"It was nothing, Annie, really," she whispered. But Annie didn't respond and she turned.

Annie was still inside the cabin, and she hadn't been talking to Melody.

She was talking to Steven.

"I'm not lying," Steven said. She could see his feet at the table.

Annie laughed. *She laughed with a man.* "Huge footprints in the stone?" she asked, animated, bright and teasing. Her sister as Melody knew her, not the silent shadow she'd been for the last year. "Am I really to believe that?"

Happiness and relief for her sister roared through Melody, like a storm rolling off the ocean. It wasn't entirely unexpected; of course she would grow comfortable enough with Steven to speak to him. Laugh with him. She'd saved his life.

It had been so long since she'd heard her sister talk to anyone the way she talked to Melody. Almost the entire ten months of their journey. But here, of course, in the safety of this beautiful clearing, her sister would blossom.

The happiness and relief were suddenly squashed with guilt. With failure.

Tears bit into Melody's eyes.

I can't secure this for you, she thought. *I can't secure it for either of us. He rejected me.*

She heard the slide and lurch of her sister's gait behind her and she stiffened, wiping her eyes.

"Melody, how is the gardening?"

"Fine. We'll finish tomorrow." She sniffed and made a big show of looking out at the clearing.

"Melody?"

Melody finally looked up into her sister's brown eyes. So familiar, those eyes. They'd been her touchstone and her compass for years. Tears spilled over her cheeks.

"What's wrong?" Annie awkwardly tried to sit and Melody helped her, holding her elbow, bracing her weight as she had a thousand times before.

"I heard you talking to Steven."

"And that made you cry?"

"It's been years since I've heard you laugh with someone, Annie. Years. " Annie took Melody's hand and squeezed it and they sat side by side, staring out at the trees, for a long time. A dizzying array of green. Dark to light, nothing uniform. "You like it here, don't you?"

"It's lovely. Quiet."

She took a deep heavy breath. "Cole offered us enough money to get home again."

"There is nothing for us there."

"That's what I told him."

"Are you apprehensive about Denver?"

If apprehensive is another word for dread, then yes.

"You're not apprehensive, are you?" Melody asked.

"A little I suppose. Largely, I am excited."

"By what?"

"All of it, I suppose. The two of us in our own home with no man to answer to. Honest work. New people. Doesn't the thought of that make you happy?"

"If you are happy, I am happy." It came out sarcastic and

she immediately regretted it.

"Stop. You have always thought happiness was something you could control through a man. You've never had to do it on your own."

"Perhaps because I have been too busy worrying about you!" she snapped.

Annie recoiled. "Why is this suddenly about me?"

"Because Denver is just like that lost little boy—"

"What are you talking about? What lost boy?"

"Remember when we were young and you told me we had a baby brother who was lost? And you had us searching the property for days looking for a little boy who did not exist?" Annie looked confused. "Of course you don't remember. You live in your head, unaware of the dangers. That's why Mama said I was to look out for you—"

"Are you talking about Mama's miscarriage?"

Melody blinked. "What?"

"Mama had a miscarriage when we were young. I think I was six, so you must have been four. I overheard Mama and Father talking about losing a boy. And I guess I thought they meant it literally."

"Mama thought you were looking for a lost imaginary friend."

"Well, that's the most illogical thing I've ever heard." Annie laughed and the sound, so rare, was contagious, and Melody found herself laughing too. Laughing until they were resting their shoulders against each other to catch their breath. "Mama never did think much of me."

"Father never thought much of me."

"That's not true."

Melody gave her sister a dubious smile.

"I think he was mystified by you, just as Mama thought I was odd because I never cared about the things she cared about. And I know everyone pitied me," Annie said. "But I have never felt pitiful. Once mother washed her hands of me ever getting married, she left me alone. Everyone left me alone. All I had to do was dress for the parties and stay away from the punch. And I had this freedom because no one cared about me. I read what I wanted. Talked to whomever I wanted. About all manner of inappropriate topics. And I found out who I was when so little was expected of me. When I had no one to please but myself."

"How novel." She could not keep the bitterness from her voice.

"Every eye was on you, and I could not understand how you flourished under that attention. But you did."

"Not all of me," she said. Not the good parts. The small, pettiest parts of her had flourished. The rest of her had starved. But out here, she found, in the clearing, with this work, these glimpses she had of simple happiness. Here she was finding parts of herself she'd forgotten about. Or perhaps never knew about.

"When the war started I was left even more alone, and then Father needed me and that freedom was galvanized with a purpose. And I like my freedom. You can have that freedom now. It's not a bad thing, Melody. It's wonderful."

"Of course it is," Melody whispered. *But what if I don't want it?*

Annie went back inside, but Melody did not get up.

They'd had a barn cat, a terrified tabby who every morning stood at the doorway and never went further. Scared of the outside world. She was that cat.

Or perhaps, she thought, the tabby wasn't terrified. Perhaps the tabby just understood that the barn was warm and safe and dry, and whatever adventure waited out in the tall grass and bushes, it was not as fine as the home she had indoors.

She had seen enough new sights. Experienced enough adventure.

She'd crossed the Mississippi river, climbed mountains, waded through a sea of prairie with grass as high as her wagon seat. She'd seen Indians and trappers. Whores and missionaries.

A man who wore the skin of a bear like a suit.

And none of it was as interesting to her as sitting still. Watching the seasons change on one piece of land. Watching what would come of the kitchen garden they'd just planted.

Yes, she thought. *I am that cat.*

And it was a sour thing to realize just as it was being taken away.

CHAPTER 12

MELODY FOUND A cherry tree, and on the south-facing branches the fruit was ripe.

Well, she thought, biting into one only to have it taste more sour than sweet, *ripe enough.*

They'd been saving the last of their vinegar in order to make more, and with this fruit they could. And she would add the stones to their seed collection.

She was so busy gathering them she did not hear Cole come up.

"What did you find?" he asked.

She started, dropping an edge of her apron, and the cherries she'd gathered scattered on the pine needles and dirt.

"Excuse me," he said, bending to help her pick them up. "I did not mean to startle you."

Their hands brushed and she could feel his breath against her hair. He was sweating, having spent the day pulling logs back into the clearing for more of his building projects.

The smell of him made her dizzy.

"These cherries aren't quite ripe," he said, spitting out a stone.

"They are ripe enough for my purpose."

"Would you like to tell me that purpose?" He was trying to tease her into pretending that nothing happened between them, but she would not play along.

She let her silence be answer enough.

"My mother used to make brandied cherries. Sweet—"

"I am making vinegar."

"Of course you are."

She stood up. "Is that a joke about my disposition?"

He stood as well, and she noticed how tired he looked. How worn. "No," he said. "It is a comment on the nature of sweet things to turn sour."

That too seemed pointed. Too pointed and she hurried to gather the rest of the cherries.

"They gave us a ration of vinegar in the war. Well, in the beginning anyway. To keep away scurvy." He continued to chat as if she had not thrown herself at him, only to be cast aside.

She stood, flustered and embarrassed. "There is no point in your pretending."

"Pretending?" He stood, his hands full of red cherries.

"Your charade is unkind."

"Melody—" She turned, but he grabbed her elbow and it felt as if she'd set her skin against the hot kettle. "This is no charade. I care for you. I like you."

"Not enough for marriage."

"Not enough for marriage with a woman who does not care for or like me. Your desperation—"

"Yes, you've made that clear. You don't like my fear. Or my worry. Or my desperation. You are like Jimmy in that regard, aren't you—"

"I am nothing like Jimmy!"

"You would have me only show you the parts of myself that you enjoy. And hide the rest of my ugly feelings—"

To her shock he grabbed her elbows, pulling her closer, so close the cherries fell again. So close she took a breath and felt his body against hers.

"I would have you show me everything, Melody. Everything." His breath, his voice, his gaze, it burned.

She yanked herself away from him, feeling as if her skin were too tight. "You forget yourself," she whispered.

"I don't think so."

"These things you want," she spat, feeling wild. Hysterical. Jimmy and Christopher's mother went mad during the war, screaming and running around in soiled clothes. Melody was a breath away from that. "There is a price to pay for them. You can't just be . . . happy. Or loved. Not without grief and pain. And I cannot stand anymore suffering! I would rather feel nothing for the rest of my life if it meant I would never again hurt so much!"

He reached for her, his face contorted with sympathy, and she smacked at his hands so hard her fingers stung. And she would have kept slapping but forced herself to step back, clench her hands in fists under her armpits.

"What if happiness and love is the reward for having survived what we've survived?" he asked.

At his words she felt her heart strain, leaping like an unbroken horse toward hope. Toward belief. Toward him.

But when she opened her mouth, laughter poured out. "Don't be such a fool."

He made an exasperated, frustrated sound in his throat, and then he picked up the saplings he'd been dragging through the wood and headed back to the clearing.

For a very long moment she stood there and caught her breath and then she knelt to once again gather her sour cherries.

CHAPTER 13

SOMETHING HAD TO be done with the mare, Lilly. She'd gone into heat and Duke and Jacks were about to kick down the barn to get to her.

Cole was not indifferent to the sentiment. Melody had built a fortress of ice around herself since that alarming scene in the forest two days ago, and he could not get through it.

He understood her pain and her fear, and with time and patience he thought he could melt that ice, but she was not giving him the chance.

"Sit," he told his brother, who lowered himself onto a stump while Cole went into the barn to get Lilly. He set her loose to graze on the tall grass and stood by his brother.

"We can make an offer to buy the mare," Steven said.

Cole agreed. "It would probably be best coming from you."

Steven looked up at Cole, but Cole couldn't read him. Steven had never been mysterious or opaque. Steven had been a bright light and now he was entirely made of dark shadows.

"Are you all right?" Cole asked. "Your head?"

"Fine."

"Your eyesight?"

"Still blurry in my left eye. I am beginning to think it will not come back."

That was true about so many things.

"What have you done to make the widow so angry?" Steven asked.

"She proposed marriage and I said no."

The old Steven would have found this situation ripe for teasing. He would have sat Cole down and interrogated him for hours, but this new Steven only lifted one eyebrow with mild interest.

"I thought you were growing fond of her."

"I am." Fond seemed such a lukewarm word for what he felt. It was lust and admiration, curiosity and respect. It was more than he'd ever felt for a person outside of his family.

"Do I need to explain how marriage works, Cole?"

"I would like to think that the woman I spend the rest of my life with, raise my family with, would . . . care for me."

"I see the war did not cure you of your romance."

"I won't be embarrassed for wanting what Mother and Father had."

Steven peeled bark from the stump and flung it off to the grass. "The widow seems a cold and calculating woman to compare to Mother."

"She is. But she's also the woman who risked everything to save your life. She's the woman who carried seeds across the country so she could plant peach trees to remind her of home." *She kissed me when she was terrified. And when I touched her she went breathless.* "Am I foolish to think she has more to her than her worry and hopelessness?"

"You're foolish to think anyone has more than that, Cole."

Cole did not agree, and it broke his heart that his brother felt that way.

"So, you are seducing the widow?" Steven asked.

"I am trying."

"Try harder and faster; they leave in a week."

MELODY CAME OUT of the cabin with a basket for the eggs and a pail for the goat's milk. She'd grown accustomed to the luxury of eggs and milk. And now with vinegar they could soon have curds again.

They would have to buy a goat and chickens in Denver.

Cole and Steven had Lilly in the field, which for some reason alarmed her. Like a child, she wanted to pull Lilly from their sight and cry, *mine!*

"What are you doing?" she asked as she approached.

"Nothing nefarious, I assure you. Lilly is going into heat," Cole said. "Duke and Jacks were about to kick apart the barn."

"Heat?" She nearly dropped the basket.

"We would like to buy Lilly from you," Steven said.

"Buy her?"

"Are you okay?" Cole asked, and she wanted to smack at him. She wanted to snarl and snap. *How much more of my life do you want? You have my seeds and now you'll have my horse? And you still want more?*

She ignored him, as she had for the last two days. He wanted more so she gave him nothing.

"We will pay you a fair price," Steven said in his level way. She felt ridiculous for her childish silence when Steven was so reasonable. And she knew, looking at them, that they would overpay her. They would give her and Annie the best possible price for Lilly. That Lilly would be better cared for here, in this beautiful meadow under the hands of these men, than with any stranger they met in Denver.

And that made her want to put her foot down and say no. Out of spite. Out of childish nastiness.

But there was no choice in the end.

"All right," she said. "I'll need to talk to my sister, but I'm sure we can sell."

She'd thought for so long that she didn't feel anything, but she felt this, a clean snap in her chest.

Lilly. Lilly would stay and she would have to leave.

She could hear the horses inside the barn. The building shook as one of them kicked the door.

"I'm going to get Duke," Cole said, and he took off at a run for the barn.

"Did my brother do something he needs to apologize for?" Steven said after Cole was gone.

"What makes you ask?"

"You aren't speaking to him."

"If he did, what would you do? Make him apologize?"

Steven smiled briefly. "He's never been made to apologize. Cole has always done the right thing."

Including refusing the advances of a widow who would force him into marriage.

"He doesn't need to apologize," she whispered.

"Somehow his romantic nature survived the war." A giant cloud covered the sun and the clearing was suddenly shadowed. "He was engaged to a girl—"

"Jane."

"He told you?"

She nodded, unable to speak.

"They'd been engaged almost his whole life. He was never interested in anyone else. Never courted anyone else, or tried to kiss—"

"What does this have to do with me?" she interrupted, not interested in the love story of Jane and Cole.

"My brother is trying to seduce you and he doesn't know how."

Overhead the cloud passed and sunlight flooded the clearing, making her eyes sting.

Cole came out of the barn with Duke, and the horse needed no goading to be sent into the clearing. Within moments Duke had mounted Lilly, a violent loud act that sent blood pounding to Melody's fingers. Behind her eyes. The whole world seemed on edge with the intimacy. Or perhaps that was just her. She turned away, not embarrassed by the act, but what it made her feel.

Twitchy and awful and sad.

More.

It made her feel more.

More was what she wanted to avoid.

Because it was painful.

MELODY HAD MENDING to do and with Steven's words in her ears, she decided to do it outside. Under the trees. Across the clearing from the garden where Cole was finishing his planting.

He is trying to seduce you and he doesn't know how.

He was so handsome. Sharp, and yet worn at the same time. There was no excess, nothing frivolous, just a man and his body and his soul.

It was days ago now, but her wrist still burned and throbbed where his thumb had been. Her body ached where his had been pressed against it.

I would have you show me everything.

She'd certainly shown him something, hadn't she? Screaming, slapping his hands. But she didn't have any embarrassment. Instead, she pitied him and his romance.

She didn't have any *more*. The freedom she'd felt after shooting Jimmy was a sham. There was no more faith left in her. She was grit and rock and bone. It had been two days since he'd touched her. Two days of the dark man she'd known a little over three weeks ago turning into...someone else. He joked and teased. Laughed.

And he played that damn harmonica and she'd wanted to weep at the stories the music told. She wanted to tell him to stop watching her. Because he did, he watched her all the time. His gaze like a touch at her back.

It was obvious now, his attempts at seduction.

She tied a knot in the thread and snapped it, the hole in Steven's shirt now a delicate barely-there seam. In time, when

Cole took her and Annie back down to Denver, this farm would be much like that shirt. You'd hardly know she and Annie had been there except for the garden. And now Lilly.

Suddenly Cole was sitting beside her, stretched out in the grass. So close, too close. She could feel him along the side of her, through the thin silk of her dress, along the bare skin of her arms. He exhaled and she felt it across her shoulders. It had been a long time since she sat so close to a man and was not afraid.

She shifted away from him, drew herself into her skin. Her body. So there was no chance he would touch her.

The sun was behind him and she had to squint when she looked at him, but still she couldn't see him clearly. He was a dark face with a white halo.

"Do you need some help?" he asked.

"You've darned a lot of socks?"

"I knew three men who had toes amputated because they started a march with a hole in their sock and ended it with blisters that festered."

"Oh . . . my." Now she felt terrible for being flippant.

"So I can fix a hole." He plucked a darning needle from her mother's small velvet pincushion, which was balanced on her knee, and wool from the socks she'd already pulled apart. She was reinforcing the cuff of his blue shirt and he pulled a black sock from the pile.

"I spoke to your brother today," she finally said when she could take the silence no more.

He was silent, watching her from the corner of his eyes.

"About rock oil refining? My brother is keen on that topic."

"No." She stabbed her needle through the blue linen, her stitches growing messy. Mama would make her pluck them out.

"Denver, perhaps? He has plans to invest in the railroad."

"Your brother did not talk about himself. He talked about you. He said you are trying to seduce me."

"I am."

"You understand that it serves my purpose to let you."

"I do."

She threw up her hands. "Then just say yes to marriage and have it be done with!"

They did not pretend to stitch. They didn't pretend to do anything but sit there, him staring at her, she staring at the frayed cuff of his blue shirt.

"That first night we met, with Jimmy in the cabin. The way I behaved, the gracious hostess, the Southern lady—that was a part I played because he wanted me to be that way. If you want me to playact at love, I can do that, too."

"Stop, please," he whispered and put his hand over hers. "I don't want you to playact at anything. I want you as you are."

Once she'd seen a spider frozen in a giant chunk of golden amber. Someone's treasure brought over to America generations ago from Europe. Right now she felt like that spider, unable to break his gaze.

"You saw how I am. By the cherry tree."

"You do not scare me, Melody. But are you afraid?" he whispered. "Of me?"

She shook her head. Slowly he leaned in, and she realized he was giving her plenty of time to move. To back away. Perhaps to slap him, but when his hand touched her face, she melted into the touch. He laid his palm against her cheek, his fingers going into her hair, and she turned into the contact. She'd asked for kindness and this seemed, somehow, its most pure form.

His lips, when they touched hers, were soft and warm. A surprising luxury on such a sparse man. Of the things she missed, she'd forgotten about kissing. Oh, she'd loved kissing. She pushed into his lips and he melted this time. He groaned and pulled her closer, opening his mouth against hers. She thought of how she'd tried to hide her experience from Christopher, who had been far from her first kiss, and Jimmy, who loved to punish her for her past, but she didn't bother with Cole.

Unlike their first kiss, Cole took charge of this one. When his tongue swept into her mouth, she met it with her own. He tasted of coffee and tooth powder and him. A delicious slick and wet heat. He pushed the pile of clothing away and pulled her closer, against him. She felt the strength and warmth of him through their clothing and gasped. The needle and shirt spilled from her grasp and she wrapped her hands around his neck, her fingers finding home in the thick hair at his nape. All of her found a home against him, the heavy weight of her breasts, the trembling muscles of her stomach, lips, teeth and tongue, all them found a welcoming spot on his body.

He lay back in the grass, pulling her over him. She felt the hard ridge of his erection against her belly, and tension made her freeze. Both of them stopped, breathing carefully through their mouths against each other.

"I am sorry," he whispered. "I . . . am carried away." He shifted to sit up, but she spread her hands wide across his shoulders.

A man who cared so diligently for seeds would not hurt her the way Jimmy had. And perhaps a man who cared so diligently for seeds would show her more pleasure than Christopher had shown her in those rushed, awkward moments.

I am not scared of you, she thought and kissed him again. He groaned, his hand sweeping down from her hair to her waist and over her hips. Fire rippled under her skin and everywhere he touched her it blazed, until she didn't know herself. She was a stranger in his arms.

The thought was exciting and she moaned, running her fingers from his shoulders to his chest, where muscles jumped under her touch. He broke the kiss and pressed his lips to her neck, so much skin revealed by that stupid ball gown and suddenly she loved that dress more than she had when it was beautiful.

He kissed her collarbones, the tender skin where shoulder met neck, the trembling tops of her breasts. Her gasp was loud in the silent meadow and his chuckle was louder.

"Are you laughing at me?" she gasped, trying for teasing but feeling stupidly like she wanted his assurance.

"Never. I am laughing at us." He rolled again, putting her on her back in the grass, her blue skirts draped over his legs. His fingertips traced her cheekbone, the corner of her lips. She gasped, her skin so sensitive she felt the ripples of his touch in her belly, her chest, down to her toes. His fingertips touched her ear and measured the pulse in her throat. His eyes, the color of soil, of healthy earth, never left hers and she felt a terrible ache bloom in her breasts. Between her legs. Restless, she arched against him, biting her lips.

His fingertips found the edge of her neckline and traced it from her shoulder to the center of her chest. His eyes left hers to look down at her body, and she stared up at the blue sky.

"You're beautiful," he whispered. "But you've been told that before."

His finger traveled over silk to the hard point of her nipple, and she tried to swallow a groan. "If we had met before the war, I don't think we would have found much to admire about each other."

She wished she could smile. She wished she could actually follow his conversation, but his fingers danced over her dress, pulling and touching and grazing. "But I find your beauty to be the least of your attractions," he continued. "I am compelled by your boldness and your strength. The darkness in you that matches the darkness in me."

His touch turned fierce, a sharp, hot pinch of her nipple, and she nearly sprang from her skin.

His eyes kindled and he squeezed her nipple again and she moaned, her teeth biting into her lip.

None of this was unfamiliar. But yet, this burning under her skin, this restless ache in her belly, it was wholly new. Cole's touch was . . . transformative. It turned her skin to water, her blood and bone to . . . something else. Lightning, perhaps.

His body was alive with heat and intent and she groaned. Overcome.

His whole hand cupped her breast and it was gentle . . . but not. Careful . . . but not. His thumb and forefinger found her nipple again and pulled, rolled it. And she turned her face away, embarrassed by her reaction, while he simply watched her.

"Don't," he breathed. "Don't look away from me."

He took her hand and put it at his neck, where she felt not just the searing heat of his skin, but the throb of his heart. "We are together in this," he said.

Together in this. It was as if a bell had been rung in her chest, and the words vibrated through her. She looked back at him, seeing the high color in his cheeks, feeling the pant of his breath.

No longer content to lie there and be touched, she pulled him down to her for another kiss.

It was wild this time, and that matched her desire fully. He sucked her tongue into his mouth, his hand swept from her breast to her hip and he rolled her toward him, and he kept her there with an arm against her back. She could not hold him hard enough, close enough. The clothes between them were too much of a barrier and she pushed her hand up under the bottom of his shirt, spreading her palm wide against the smooth skin of his back.

He hissed and kissed her as if he wanted to devour her.

The muscles of his back danced under his skin.

His hand dropped to her leg and he began to pull up her skirt.

"Cole." Steven's voice was as sharp as a gunshot across the meadow, and Cole stopped. Melody felt like screaming. He broke the kiss and pressed her head to his neck.

"Are you all right?" he asked her.

Dying of mortification, she thought, but nodded.

"Give us a second, Steven," Cole said, and she risked a look under his arm at Steven, only to find him standing there with Annie.

She groaned and buried her face in Cole's neck.

He got up and helped her to her feet. The weight of three people watching her was overwhelming, and scalding tears of embarrassment burned behind her eyes. Head down, mortified, she gathered the clothing that had been scattered.

Cole helped, smiling all the while.

"This is funny?" she asked.

"A little." He winked at her and she wanted to smack him. "My brother is going to scold me."

"That . . . that is all you have to say?" She glared at him. "This wasn't enough *more*?" She spat the word as if it were poison. And it was to her.

His face got hard, but she would not apologize. He knew her intentions.

"It wasn't the right more," he said.

She walked away from him, the clothes clutched in her arms, forcing herself to hold her head high as she walked past Steven and her sister.

Inside, she put the clothing down on the table and waited for Annie to arrive with her worry. Frantic, she tried to focus herself by folding the clothes.

"What are you doing, Melody?" Annie asked from the doorway. "What scheme is this?"

"There is no scheme—"

"Stop lying to me!" Annie was undone, shaking, blushed with fury.

"I proposed."

"Marriage?"

"Don't worry, he rejected."

Annie's gasp was censorious and shocked. Another lifetime ago, Melody would have rolled her eyes. But now she felt too used to play her part in this scene. "Then what was that?"

Melody shook her head. She was making a mess of the folding and so she stopped, her hands limp and useless on the table. "I'm not sure."

"You're more than just your assets as a wife. Or a whore."

Melody flinched at the word from her sister's mouth. "I know that, Annie. But I got carried away. I've heard it happens."

"Have you been carried away with Cole before?"

"No. Calm down, Annie, I am fine."

"Steven will make Cole do the right thing."

"It was a kiss, Annie. That's all. Don't be such a prude."

"You think I disapprove of sex. I only disapprove of how you use it to secure a future neither of us want!"

"I want it!" she cried, and then bit her lips, shaking her head.

"What are you talking about?"

"I want this life. I want this clearing and this work. I want a family. Children." *And Cole.*

But he would not marry her.

"But . . . what of Denver?"

"Denver is your dream, Annie. Not mine."

"And you would go behind my back to make sure it doesn't happen?"

"I'm sorry," she sighed.

"Sorry?" Annie cried. "As if that makes it okay? I thought you saw me, Melody. I thought you knew me, but you are just like Mama and all the rest—"

"Annie . . .?"

"This is so like you. To believe you know best because I couldn't possibly be able to keep us safe. I couldn't possibly want something besides orbiting your much brighter star. I couldn't possibly have an idea about our future, *my* future. You would rather put yourself at risk than trust your odd, crippled sister—"

"That isn't it!"

"Stop lying to yourself and to me."

"Listen to me. Perhaps . . . perhaps you are right. I didn't trust your plan, not because of your leg, but because I'm not you. I do not want what you want, and you're right, I did go behind your back, but it hardly matters. He said no."

"Only you would say it hardly matters," Annie whispered. "As if betraying me was nothing worse than a punch stain on a gown."

She could feel her sister's anger and it was far more than a sulk. Melody felt miniscule. Too tiny to be seen. They would leave and in Denver she would go numb, and at this moment that sounded better than staying and being hurt.

"Perhaps it's best if we left soon," Melody said.

"Perhaps it is" , Annie snapped, the fight far from over.

CHAPTER 14

"WE APPRECIATE YOUR kindness," Annie said later that night as they ate supper on the porch. The sunset was a blaze of pink and orange over the mountains. Melody put down her fork, unable to eat. "But we think it would be best if we left. Soon."

Melody heard the scrape of plates and forks stop as Cole and Steven both turned to stare at Annie and then at her.

"We would like to leave tomorrow." Annie nodded. "Two days at most."

Melody's blood vessels carried fire and remorse. Her skin, she knew, was red as a cherry, and she could do nothing to stop it but lift her chin and stare right at the sunset, hurting her eyes.

"That is what you want?" Steven asked, as if the answer might change.

"It would be best. We have our future to think of."

Yes. Our beautiful future of numb loneliness. Melody felt the food she'd eaten well up in her throat. It did not matter that numb loneliness was what she wanted.

"Melody?" Steven asked. Finally she turned, and both of the men were staring at her.

Cole's silence was damning. His eyes unreadable. He sat there . . . impervious.

Your darkness that matches mine.

She would find someone else. Someone who didn't require so much of her. Who didn't make her laugh and cry and want things that were beyond her reach.

"I want to leave," she said.

"Cole." Steven stared daggers into his brother. "You will allow this?"

Cole nodded. "It is her choice."

"Do you see?" Steven barked, angrier than she'd ever seen him. "Do you see what comes of love? This is not our life before the war, brother. You don't get to be romantic about this."

Cole was silent.

Love? Melody shook her head. Love was making a mess of all of them.

Steven blew out a long breath and hung his head. "All right, I guess . . . tomorrow Cole will fill a barrel at the seeps. The next morning he will take you to Denver. The money from the oil, combined with what we agree on for Lilly, and what I will pay you gaze saving my life, will buy you a house. Money left over from that, if you are careful, will last you a while."

"I plan to seek work with one of the doctors in town." Annie's eyes were alight in a way Melody had never seen.

"I know Dr. Meadows; I will write you a letter of introduction," Steven offered.

As they talked about this doctor, Melody stared down at her hands, at the blisters that had callused after the planting, until she was unable to pretend to be indifferent any longer.

When she looked right at Cole it was to find him silently watching her.

You will let me leave? Just like that?

His gaze was unreadable and she forced herself not to manufacture his thoughts. If he could not tell her what he thought, than it did her no good to try and guess.

I do not want to go. But she had so few means with which to control her life.

"I am not hungry," she said, and took her plate into the cabin.

After dinner there was no music. Steven and Cole went out to the barn, and bitterness brewed between Melody and her sister.

"You should have made the plans all along," Melody said, running her cracked and blistered fingers against the smooth buttons of her dress.

"What plans?"

"The plans for us. You are far more capable than I am. Far more—"

"Stop."

"No." She turned toward her sister, lost in the shadows on the far side of the room. "It's true. I have only ever wanted a home. A family. You are the one with ambition."

"There will be a home for us in Denver," Annie said. "And I let you make the plans, Melody, because you were so much more fearless. And I was so used to not speaking up."

Melody nodded, though the ache in her chest would not go away.

She said nothing else as they dressed for bed, through the quiet hush of Steven and Cole returning from the barn, the crackle of someone stirring the fire.

And now, in the silent cabin, she felt her future pressing in on her. Suffocating her. Did Annie feel like this every time Melody made a decision for them? Did this resentment and frustration crackle through her?

How stupid I was to think I needed to care for her. She is a thousand times more capable than I am.

Melody threw off her blankets.

But it wasn't enough. She still couldn't breathe. Denver loomed in her mind.

Melody stood and grabbed Annie's wrap from the nail near the door. She would go outside, say goodbye to Lilly. The garden. The view from the porch.

The other room was cozy in the last of the crackling firelight, and she was surprised to see Cole sitting up at the table, watching the flames. Silently they stared at each other, her heart pounding so loudly she was sure he could hear it. She was sure it would wake up Steven and Annie.

Cole stood from his chair, his shirt untucked and unbuttoned, as if he'd been distracted while undressing. Firelight danced over the skin of his belly and chest, and her fingers twitched with the desire to touch him. To slide her hands around his muscled rib cage to his back.

He crossed the small distance between them, walking out of the firelight and into the shadows. His nearness made her ache, and she was aware of the slickness between her legs. How her lungs couldn't quite gather in enough air.

"Follow me," he breathed. He turned for the door, lighting the lamp and gathering blankets as he went.

Her heart pounded with victory. Her fingers went numb.

He meant to compromise her. She wasn't stupid. This wasn't goodbye. And she would be compromised.

But when Cole followed up whatever liberties he took—and she allowed—by coming up to scratch, it would mean marrying a man who would always be disappointed. Who would always want something from her that she did not know how to give.

Am I that strong? she wondered.

If it meant staying in this meadow and not going to Denver, she would do it. She would be compromised, insist he do the right thing and then suffer the consequences of marriage to a man she was doomed to disappoint.

She thought briefly of Annie, of their diverging paths, of an uncertain future, but she found she had to make this choice, here and now, for herself. Annie would go to Denver and she would stay.

For her own happiness.

She'd done wrong things before. Bad things. Scandalous things.

But following Cole out that door and across the clearing to the barn, she felt no guilt.

Inside the small cave Cole put down the blankets and the lamp.

Behind him, she put her hand to his back, felt the muscles under his shirt bunch at her touch. Growing bolder, she put both hands against his shoulder and reached forward to his chest to grab the neck of the shirt and pull it down his arms.

"Melody—"

He turned, but she didn't give him a chance to talk. On tiptoes and still too short, she reached to kiss him, tugging him to meet her halfway. His lips, their surprising voluptuousness, were perfectly familiar after just a few kisses. She'd kissed Christopher a hundred times, and while she'd enjoyed it, she had no memory of his lips, no impression. Ten years from now she would remember the surprise of Cole's lips. He tensed as if to push her away, but she'd been here before and knew what to do when a man would try to be reasonable, when she needed him unreasonable.

She dropped Annie's wrap from her shoulders and stepped into Cole's chest, her breasts pressed against Cole's naked chest through the thin lawn of her nightgown, and she gasped at the sensation, the liquid rush of desire that flooded through her.

His hands gripped her elbows and she twined her arms around his neck, giving him no chance to push her away. She kissed him as she liked to be kissed. She licked at his lips, and when he didn't let her in, she took his lower lip between her teeth and nipped at him. He jumped and then laughed, a low rumble. Her tongue swept in, laying claim. He dropped her elbows and eased his hands into her hair. She braced herself to be pushed away, but instead he tilted her head, finding a better angle, and when his tongue swept into her mouth, it was deep, rough. And she tasted something different in him. In them, perhaps. Something wild . . . but resolute.

Her hands skated over his flesh, across dips and valleys, muscle and the fur of his chest. A thousand variations on a masculine theme and she had never, ever enjoyed touching someone so much. Her fingertips brushed the skin just over the tops of his pants and he flinched away from her. Again, laughing.

For such a serious man he sure found kissing to be joyful.

His thick, calloused fingers tugged loose the three small buttons at the top of her gown. Cool air touched her chest, the curve of her breasts, the tops of her arms. He stepped back and pushed the rest of the gown off her body. She knew her body was pleasing, though it was thinner than it had ever been and she had muscles where before she'd only had soft, round flesh. But Cole gazed at her like she was heaven solidified.

And in the lamplight, he looked heavenly as well. Strong and lean and solid. She touched the muscles of his stomach, her fingertips dancing over the ridges. His hand touched her breast, followed the slope to her nipple, and she found the distance between them was not to her liking. She pulled him closer, met him halfway, hungry for more of his surprising mouth, and he obliged, bending his head to kiss her. His hands cupped her breasts, skated over her waist. Down over her hips to curve around her bottom. She gasped against his lips, surprised at the touch, and he pulled her closer, harder. And the anger simmering in her veins, her powerlessness over her life, found a brilliant release and she arched against him harder, rubbing herself against the erect flesh in his pants. He groaned and dropped his mouth to her neck, pressing open-mouthed kisses to her throat, her chest and then, to her surprise, he pulled her nipple into his mouth through the thin cotton of her nightgown. She jumped and gasped, her fingernails biting into his skin.

Her violence begat his and he used his teeth against her and shocking sharp pleasure rippled and unfurled and she found herself pushing harder against him. Wanting more from him.

Bolder than she'd ever been, she reached her hand between them and pressed into the front of his pants. Surely he would understand and take it from there. But no, he seemed content to lick and suck her breasts, making her crazy. Mad.

"Cole," she gasped.

He dropped to his knees on the ground, pressing hot, wet kisses to her stomach. His tongue touched her belly button, dipped inside.

She jumped away, but he held her, his hands at her bottom. And she could not move.

He breathed against the brown hair between her legs and she twitched, again trying to get away from him.

"What are you doing?"

"This isn't something you've done before?"

She wanted to tell him that most of her experience involved kissing, a hand at her breast and varying degrees of discomfort. This was wholly new.

"No," she breathed. "Who does this?"

"I do."

And then he touched her. There. Not just on the hair. But inside. Inside where she could feel her own wetness. His finger slipped along the fold of her, to the entrance of her body, and she felt a breathless . . . absence. As if she wanted that finger inside of her, but instead he slipped away, to the top of her fold. Where the knot of nerves she was so often aware of while kissing, or horseback riding or dancing—waited.

The calloused edge of his finger against the knot made her jerk, and the entire inside of her body felt that touch. And then he did it again. And again, long slow slides that both hurt and felt good.

"I don't . . . I don't like that," she said.

"Give it a second," he breathed, his attention locked on

her. His finger moved faster, his other hand spread her open a bit and she knew he was watching. She lifted her eyes to the ceiling and wondered why he couldn't just be more like Christopher, let her trap him into marriage and be done with it.

But then, suddenly, there was another sensation and she looked down to see him kissing her. There. And his finger . . . oh, his finger was inside of her. And the knot of nerves was being tormented by his tongue, and she couldn't feel her legs any longer, and the top of her skull was tingling and the ground seemed to move beneath her feet and something . . . something was happening. Something wild and scary, and she pushed at his shoulders, but he gripped her harder, closer. His tongue, his fingers, that wicked, wicked mouth of his would not be deterred, and suddenly she was crying out and falling and breaking apart. And it was terrifying and wonderful all at the same time.

"Cole!" she cried, and bent forward, over him. Her hand was in his hair, pressing him to her, and then he was helping her, easing her down onto his lap, her legs spread over his bent knees, her face buried in his neck.

Slowly, he ran his hand up and down her back, over her spine in big wide swaths. Tears bit into her eyes. She'd never been so undone and then so comforted. Ever.

"That's never happened before," she said.

"Did you like it?"

She laughed and nodded, her face still in the warm crease of his neck. He was sweating and she sipped at where moisture had gathered in the tendons of his shoulder. She kissed his collarbone. The top of his chest. The fur there tickled her nose and she pressed her whole face into him.

His breathing hitched and beneath her she felt his erection.

"Can I . . . I would like to do that to you," she said.

Cole swore under his breath.

"You don't want that?"

"I want that very much."

He carefully moved her off his lap and set her down on the ground.

On her knees beside him, she fumbled with the buckle to his belt and he took off his pants, easing them down his legs. His erection was pink and hard, rising up from a dark cloud of hair, arching up against his belly. He braced one hand behind him and put the other around his erection.

He stroked it and she felt desire build in her again. This was so base. So raw . . . but also . . . so exciting. It was as if he were showing her everything. There were no secrets in this. No pretenses. It was in fact the most honest she'd been in years.

We are together in this. That's what he'd said, and she understood that completely in this moment.

No other intimacy in her life had been like this.

"What do you call it?" she asked, suddenly emboldened by this freedom.

"A cock."

She said the word and he groaned. Smiling, she said it again. And then her fingers touched the head of his cock, over his fist. It was soft and damp from a small hole at the top. His whole body jerked.

"This . . . " He laughed. "This will not take long."

She shook her head, unhappy with that idea. "I want it to take all night," she whispered. "The day, too." Hours, days of this freedom would not be enough.

This was the sort of freedom she longed for. Her sister could go out in the world, make her own way. She wanted to stay in this barn and map this pleasure. Map this country of sensation between them.

He bit his lip, arching against her hand. His fingers took hers, showed her what he liked. The rough touch. The squeeze at the bottom. He showed her how to gather the dampness from the top and spread it over the thick stem of him.

"Lick your hand," he told her. And she did, staring into his eyes as she did it. He was beautiful with his desire.

Her palm wet, she put it back over him and that helped, but it dried up too soon and she lifted her hand to lick it again, but he grabbed her wrist and pushed her hand down.

"Use what's between your legs," he whispered.

Oh, the fire in her was so hot. And everything between them was feeding it. She put her fingers in the slit between her legs, gasping at the touch.

"Have you ever done that?" he whispered.

"What?" she gasped, having found that knot of nerves that he'd used to bring her that stunning release.

"Touched yourself like that."

She shook her head.

"Next time," he breathed and took her hand again, applying her slippery fingers back to his cock.

"Faster," he told her. The muscles of his belly were clenching and releasing. She could hear his breath sawing in his lungs. "Harder." He groaned and she, so excited, couldn't stop staring at him.

He cried out her name and grabbed her hand, holding it hard against him, and she felt a sudden gush of hot liquid in her palm.

For a few moments the only sound was their panting. And then he found his shirt and used it to wipe up her hands, the slick stain on his belly.

She sat on her knees next to him feeling . . . undone. Cracked and broken in places. The great bravery required of her right now was not in trusting this man. Trusting Cole was easy. It was trusting herself that was the problem.

"I lied," she whispered.

"When?"

"I am not barren inside." She could not look at him. In fact, she had to turn away, sudden strange tears rising up in her eyes. This was the truth she had to be so cold to protect. But he touched her chin, forcing her to look at him.

"I do feel more. I feel so much more, but . . . " Her voice broke. Her eyes closed. "I'm so scared."

He grabbed her arms, his face suddenly fierce, his hands rougher than she'd ever experienced. She gasped, caught by him.

"What do you want, Melody?" She blinked, stunned, and he gave her a little shake. "This is not a hard question. Tell me what you want."

"To . . . care for my sister—" But even as she said it, it wasn't the truth. Not anymore. Annie did not need her care.

"You. Melody. For yourself. What do you want?"

You.

It was a whisper in the back of her head, a ludicrous thing to say and she would not say it. Could not.

I want to be who I am when I'm with you.

I want you to kiss me again. Hold me. Touch me. Everything I feel I want you to make real in my body.

I want to feel a happiness greater than my fear of pain.

"I want to stay," she said.

"Why? Because you are scared? Desperate?"

"No. Because I like it here. I am safe here. Happy. Here."

"With me?"

Oh, she burned. Horrified anger stiffened her limbs, hardened her heart. "What games do you play at, Cole?" she snapped. "I asked you to marry me."

"Why didn't you ask my brother? You must have thought about it. Considered which brother would be the most grateful, the easiest to manipulate into offering his hand."

She struggled to pull out of his hands, but he held her firm and she glared at him, panting.

"Tell me why me," he whispered, leaning into her face. His brown eyes pierced her skin and she did not have any protection against him. "Why me?"

"Because you handed me that gun! You gave me the key to

my own freedom," she cried. "And I like the way you are with the seeds. I like the way you played the harmonica. And when you looked at me I thought . . . I thought you saw me. All of me, the way no one ever has. And I thought I saw you. And I liked everything I saw."

His hands gentled on her arms, easing up to cup her shoulders and then her face. Her hair was tangled in his fingers but it was such a small pain it barely registered in all of the pain she was feeling.

"I would be honored to marry you," he murmured.

Stunned, she blinked. "You will?"

"You brought me out here to force my hand, didn't you? I am just doing what you want."

"I rescind my hand."

"That I cannot allow."

"I will not marry a man who cares nothing for me. I have done that once before."

"You think I care nothing for you?" His eyes blazed and she realized she'd made him angry. Angry enough that he reminded her of the man who first came into this clearing. The bounty hunter.

"I'm sure I don't know—"

"You took care of my brother. You took care of your sister. You brought seeds across this country to remind you of home. And you shared them with me. You lay down in the flowers and I wish more than I can say that I had lain down with you. I am astounded by you. Amazed. I've never met a woman as strong as you. As beautiful as you. You made me dream again, Melody. You made me remember the good things buried beneath all the bad. For that alone I am yours. I willingly walked into your trap, Melody."

She crossed her arms over her chest, unembarrassed that she'd done what she could to try and control her fate. She was a woman and this was the means she had available to her. "I don't find any of this funny."

"I am not laughing."

"You're smiling as if you know something I don't."

"I'm happy." He took her hand and put it on his chest, where she felt the hard thump of his heart. "I am told people smile when they are happy."

She lifted her fingers to his mouth, touching the dimples caused by his smile. He lifted his hands to hers and forced the ends into a small curve until the smile became real and she laughed into his hand.

"Why did you make me wait?"

"I didn't want you to choose me because you were scared of the alternatives. Perhaps it was pride, but I want more than that."

"More," she whispered. "You are keen on that word."

His kiss told her just how keen he was. Just how unfinished this act was between them. She wrapped her arms around his neck hard, her breasts pressed against his chest, and he groaned. His tongue swept deep into her mouth and between her legs she ached with emptiness.

He pushed her away. "I want to tell our family before I make love to you," he said. "I want to give you the chance to be married in a church in Denver, if that is what you want."

"I want you, Cole. I want . . . to make love to you. I am no virgin you need to protect."

A soft breath of air escaped him and he cupped her face in his hand. "If I could stop you from ever thinking that sort of thing again, I would."

She sat there on her knees, clutching his face, and all she wanted was to kiss him. Those lips . . . she was fascinated by those lips. Years of kissing them and she would not be satisfied.

She put her fingers into his dark, silky hair, patting it down in places, as her mother had done with her father.

She thought of her life before, of all that comfort that she'd loved. And how she had never, not in her worst nightmares, ever guessed at how fragile it all was. And now, in this cave, all too painfully aware of how hard it had been just to survive, she felt her happiness so acutely she couldn't breathe for its unexpected beauty.

"Is this love?" she whispered.

"Maybe. Maybe the beginning of it." He kissed her nose and her cheeks. Her eyelids fluttered shut as he ran his lips over her eyelashes. "Perhaps we are preparing the seeds. The soil."

"Having faith in the weather?" She laughed.

"I have faith in you," he whispered, and it was the most beautiful thing anyone had ever said to her.

"I have faith in you, too."

Their kiss was sweet. Sweeter than honey.

"My sister . . ."

"Stays with us. She's your family, I know how important she is."

"I don't think that's what she wants," she said.

"She would go to Denver alone?"

"She is strong and ambitious. And I think she has her own happiness in mind."

He kissed the top of her head and held her close, as if he could sense her sadness. "Let's go back inside."

They gathered up their things. He left off his shirt and she could not stop touching the skin of his shoulders and arms. Pressing good bye kisses to his chest.

"Already you are making this difficult," he murmured.

Hand in hand they walked back toward the cabin, where Steven and Annie were still asleep as if nothing had happened. The urge to wake up her sister and tell her that she was . . . happy, or at least hopeful. . . for the first time in years, was nearly overwhelming. But after one last goodnight kiss she slipped into bed with her sister and she stared at the ceiling, clutching her news and her hope to her chest, and fought back tears.

Because the cost of choosing Cole and this clearing was that she would lose Annie.

"I'M SORRY." ANNIE looked from Melody to Cole and back again. "What did you say?"

Melody pushed aside the coffee to grip her sister's hand. "Cole and I are getting married—"

Annie stood. A coffee cup tipped over and fell onto the ground. "I . . . w . . . w . . . w—"

The stammer, gone for so long, came back and it was alarming to see her sister so upset.

"Annie, calm down."

"I will not!" she screamed. Shaken, Melody gaped at her sister. Annie did not yell. Ever.

"We'll . . . we'll leave you alone," Cole said, helping Steven to his feet and then out of the cabin. At the doorway he stopped to smile at Melody, and she felt the ties of their connection double. It had been like that all morning. Every glance, every word she felt in her stomach and heart. A longing. For him. Not just for his lips, or that magic that he'd wrought in her body last night, but for conversations. For stories from his childhood. Why didn't he like honey? Who taught him the harmonica?

She wanted to know him.

And she wanted to tell him about riding bareback across the beach, the wind and salt and sea surrounding her. How she loved strawberries and hated asparagus. She was terrified of storms but loved the ocean. About the dark nights alone in the house with Annie during the war, clutching the rifle in her arms.

She wanted to open herself up and show him the treasures she had hidden and forgotten about.

"I'll be right outside," he said, and then stepped out onto the porch with his brother, shutting the door behind him.

"H . . . has he p . . . proposed?"

She'd lost her innocence years ago, but last night Cole had found some of it and handed it back to her. "He said yes to mine."

"D . . . id you have your dress on when he said yes?"

Melody gasped, shocked, and then she had to look away, so stunned, so terribly, horribly wounded.

"I'm sorry," Annie said, reaching across the table for her hand, and Melody stood so fast the chair fell down behind her. She jerked away from her sister's touch.

"I suppose you have every right to think that," she said, blinking back the tears. "But I never thought you would say such a thing to me."

"I spoke out of anger. I want to go to Denver."

"I know." When they were children they used to go to the riverbanks after the rain and slide down the mud. Her heart felt like that. Sliding. Down.

"I can be whatever I want there." Tears stood out in Annie's eyes, and Melody could not bear to see her sister's pain. "I can be whoever I want there. I could get a job. Be useful."

"Then you should go."

"Without you?"

"This was going to happen eventually, wasn't it? The two of us finding our own way? I have always needed you, but maybe, maybe what you've needed is to be away from me."

Annie blinked as if stunned, and Melody understood. She was stunned to be saying it.

"He means so much to you? So quickly?"

Melody circled the table and grabbed Annie's hands. Pressing them to her cheeks, the decision that was going to be made so painful she could barely stand it, but neither could she bear not to make it.

"I am falling in love with him, Annie." It was more faith than anything—the feeling was simply too new to bear the weight of a name. But she wanted it to be love. "It's more than I've ever felt. And I can't...I can't bear to think of not being with him."

Annie's hand cupped her cheek. "I'm so glad for that."

"It will be okay," Melody whispered, and they clung together in silence. Their familiar oath broken.

"YOU LOVE HER?" Steven asked as Cole paced in front of the porch.

Annie was in there right now, convincing Melody to go to Denver, and Cole didn't know how to stop it. Or if he could. What had felt so secure in the cave last night was in danger of being pulled apart. Melody had sacrificed everything for her sister; there was a very good chance he could be pushed aside.

"Is that so hard to believe?"

Steven shrugged. "It's been three weeks."

"I knew the moment she took that gun from my hand." It was the truth. This feeling in his chest, this fire, the spark was that moment. That terrible moment of faith and trust. And it had only grown until it filled this whole clearing.

"You are worrying over nothing. Melody will convince Annie to stay."

"You think?"

Steven shrugged and Cole wanted to throw his hands in the air.

"I feel like . . . everything I wanted in my life is gone. And I've come to understand that, Steven. Mother and Father, Sam and Gavin, the orchard, the work I loved—it's gone. But here, we could have something new. Something that's ours. And it feels familiar, but different. In the best way. And she feels familiar and different, but in the best way. As if I know her, but I don't. And I want to. I want to spend the next hundred years of my life knowing her. That doesn't make sense, does it?"

"No. But I like that you feel it. I like that you feel anything. I'm . . . envious."

Cole turned to face his brother. "What do you want,

Steven?"

His silence seemed impossible, hopeless. Sad.

"You survived that war for something."

"Did I?" Steven shook his head and looked out over the garden. "I just want everyone to be safe. Melody, you. Annie. I want everyone here and safe."

It broke Cole's heart to know Steven would not get that.

The door opened and the women stood there, their arms around each other's waists, their faces red with tears. And he knew in the list of things that might factor into her decision, he barely made an impression, but he suddenly needed to stand up. Be heard.

"If you go to Denver, I'll go with you," he said, drawing everyone's attention. "I woke up this morning happy. For the first time in more than six years, I was happy. Because you were here. And I could see your face and make you smile. I thought I'd walk you over to the high meadow and we could pick out a place to build a house. Build a life. Start something new. Untouched by all the ugliness in our pasts. And I want that, Melody. I want that with you. But if you want to go to Denver, we can do that there."

On the porch, Melody and Annie were slack-jawed, and he felt himself shaking. Suddenly Steven was there, beside him, the press of his shoulder against his own, shoring him up when he would falter.

Family. Everything he wanted was right on this porch, and he could not believe he'd survived all he'd survived to find it, only to lose it.

"I'm not going to Denver," Melody said.

Cole closed his eyes with relief.

"But I am," Annie said, and his eyes popped back open.

"What?" Steven asked.

"I'm going to Denver."

"By yourself?" Steven asked. "Alone?"

Annie nodded, smiling. Melody's eyes filled with tears

again, but she tried to smile too and he longed, absolutely ached, to pull her into his arms.

"I'll go," Melody said. "See her settled, but then . . . I'll come back. Because I woke up happy this morning, too. Because I want to know everything there is to know about you, Cole. And I want you to know everything about me. The bad and the good and the things I've forgotten about. And I want that here."

He held out his hand, knowing he really didn't have the right to ask her for anything, but she walked across the porch right into his arms. The delicate strength of her matched all the spots in him that had been burned out. Where he was weak, she made him strong.

He hoped he did the same for her.

Steven and Annie were arguing, but he turned Melody away, giving them all some privacy.

"I wish you did not have to choose between your sister and me—"

"I'm not," she said, looking up at him with tears in her eyes. "I'm choosing between my sister and me. I'm choosing myself, what I want. I want you. Us. A life here. And she is doing the same for herself."

He touched a tear as it slipped from her eye to her cheek. They ran faster and faster and he could not catch them all. They ran over his fingers, bathing his hands. He bent his head to kiss them away.

"If I could stop your sadness—"

"It is happiness, too," she whispered. "I am happy here. And I don't know that I've ever known this kind of happiness. But she is my sister—" Her voice broke, and he held her as hard as he could against his chest.

"Denver is a three-day ride," he said. "We will visit. Often. She can come stay with us at any time. For any amount of time."

"Promise?"

"I promise. I knew love before the war," he murmured into her hair. "It was comforting and easy and I took it for granted. What I feel for you is not comforting, or easy—it is sharp and alive and it . . . it fills me up, Melody. I could never take this for granted," he whispered.

"Good," she said, wrapping her fingers in his shirt. "Because I am not a woman who would enjoy being taken for granted."

"You're not going to stop her?" Steven cried out, and Melody and Cole turned to face them. "You are going to let her go to Denver. Alone."

Cole felt Melody crumple against him and he held her as hard as he could, giving her strength. Support.

"Her adventure is just beginning," Melody said, smiling at her sister through her tears. Steven threw up his hands and stepped off the porch, heading for the barn. Annie watched him go and then shrugged before going back inside.

"Our adventure is beginning, too," she said, and kissed Cole.

They stood on the edge of a vast, unknowable frontier. Their lives would be dangerous and unpredictable, and sorrow would no doubt visit them time and time again. But they were together, and that created more than enough light to banish all the darkness.

Dear Reader,

Thank you so much for picking up Seduced: Into The Wild Book 1. I hope you enjoyed Cole and Melody's journey back to love and life. Annie and Steven's book, TEMPTED, will be available later this year.

I love to hear from readers. You can sign up for my newsletter to find out about new releases and receive my The Author Is…interview series at www.molly-okeefe.com

Come find me on Facebook at https://www.facebook.com/MollyOKeefeBooks and Twitter at https://twitter.com/MollyOKwrites

If you have a moment, please review this book. Reviews help readers find books and I appreciate all of them, negative or positive.

Also, look for the Boys of Bishop my contemporary romance series:

Wild Child
Never Been Kissed
Between The Sheets
Indecent Proposal

Turn the page to read an excerpt from Never Been Kissed about Brody Baxter, a dangerous loner turned bodyguard, hired to save Ashley Montgomery, a woman from his past he's never been able to forget.

CHAPTER 1

Cook's Bay, Moorea, Polynesian Islands
July 2013

FOR A MAN of few words Brody Baxter hated silence.

Watching the waves crash on the beach, he wished his brother were there. Sean's chatter would make him focus.

At this point, the third hour in a four-hour shift with nothing but moonlight and dolphins in the ocean in front of the villa, Brody prayed for a three-man paramilitary attack from the water but would settle for camera-wielding paparazzi jumping out from the Tiare bush to his left.

Anything to break up the monotony.

Funny, but at one time he'd thought guarding shady politicians would be more exciting than guarding the earnest ones, but the years had taught him otherwise.

The screen door behind him slid open with a gasp and a swish. The short hair on his neck prickled in warning, but he didn't turn around. It was the woman Senator Rawlings had brought. Gina Bassili. The smell of sweat over perfume preceded her.

"Sorry," Gina said, her voice gaspy and rough. "I forgot

you were out here."

That's the idea, he thought, and stepped farther into the shadows of the balcony.

Perhaps knowing he was out here, she'd have second thoughts about enjoying the view from the balcony.

But no, the woman came to lean against the railing overlooking the bay. Her robe, barely tied at her waist, looked like a dark oil spill over her body. The color blended with her hair. The night sky behind her.

Quickly, he glanced away. She'd been loud in that villa. Lots of *Oh, Daddy*s.

"Is all this really necessary?" she asked, waving her hand around to indicate him and the other members of the team, silently guarding the senator and, by proximity, her. Her accent was nearly non-existent, but the alleys of Cairo clung to her vowels.

She'd come into the senator's life suddenly. A friend of a friend of an aide at some political fundraiser in D.C. Brody didn't particularly like how much they didn't know about her.

Choosing not to answer, Brody scanned the edge of the cliff to his left. If Brody was lucky, Senator Rawlings' wife would come rappelling over the edge with a submachine gun and he wouldn't have to engage in this conversation.

There were days he really missed the Marine Corps.

Out of the corner of his eye he saw her run her fingers over the silk edge of her robe, revealing her collarbone, the gravity-defying inside curve of her breast.

"Maybe Doug sent himself the death threats, just so he could take me someplace."

Doubtful. Brody's team didn't come cheap. And Cook's Bay was a lot of effort for a woman who probably would have put on the very same show at Four Seasons in Washington, D.C.

"Does it bother you? Listening to us?" She tipped her head, her dark hair falling down her neck. "Knowing he has a wife. A family. That he's cheating? Lying?" Her eyes glowed with a certain avarice. Obviously, it turned her on. The dirty illicitness of it. Of her role in it. It explained why she was putting on a show for a man twice her age, three times her weight, and with the morality of a shark.

For a moment he thought about telling her she was the cleanest thing in Senator Rawlings' life. That the death threats could have come from the full spectrum of extremist groups, the product of a lifetime of double dealing and lying in the name of politics.

But, lately, Rawlings was pissing off the Yetarzikstan Ba'ath party, with vocal support of the rebels.

All of this he didn't bother explaining to her, because he doubted she cared. Instead, he looked back over the ocean. The dolphins, the moonlight. *Bother him?* As a rule, Brody didn't get bothered.

"Gina?" The senator yelled from inside the door.

She shrugged, her lips twisted in coy regret.

"Duty calls," she whispered and vanished back into the villa.

The world issued an open invitation to humanity to fail itself. To be selfish and small. Mean, even evil at times. And most people, in Brody's experience, found it impossible to turn down that invitation.

The senator and his lies were just another example in a long line.

His earpiece buzzed in the split second before he heard Colin's voice. "Brody? Roy is coming up on your six. You have a visitor at HQ."

A visitor? Here?

Suddenly he thought of Ed, sick and alone in that house. Too stubborn to ask for help if he needed it.

Christ.

He and Sean should have gotten him a nurse. They'd been talking about it, but Ed was so stubborn and, in the end,

Brody didn't know how to fight him. Or maybe he just didn't care enough.

But Sean didn't know where Brody was, or how to find him.

No one did.

So not Ed.

His diaphragm relaxed.

Roy, a thick squat man Brody had worked with for years and managed to know nothing about, came up through the shadows. They nodded at each other and Brody slipped down the path through the ferns and wild banana trees to the guesthouse, where the team had set up headquarters.

Tropical bugs hovered around the light of the guesthouse veranda. To the left of the light and the cloud of bugs stood a man sweating through an expensive white button-down shirt, his suit jacket tossed over the railing. Brody couldn't get a good look at the guy's face, because his head was bent as he rolled his sleeves.

The intricate warning system of adrenaline, his gut and the hair on the back of his neck began to buzz. Whoever this guy was, he'd gone to great lengths to find Brody.

And people didn't work so hard to bring good news.

"You're here for me?" Brody asked, stepping to the edge of the light, but no farther.

"Brody Baxter?" the man asked, peering into the shadows where Brody with his dark skin and dark clothes blended into the night.

Something niggled in the back of his head. A memory. This guy wasn't a stranger. His all-American, confident-of-his-place in-the-world looks were familiar.

"Yes," Brody answered.

"You're not an easy man to find."

Once again, that is sort of the idea. Brody cut through the bullshit. "Who are you?"

"It's been a few years," the man said with a weary smile and held out his hand. "I'm Harrison Montgomery."

Brody felt deep ripples of recognition, memories of this guy and his kid sister came running from the corners where he'd shoved them years ago.

Ashley.

Brody shook Harrison's hand. Last time Brody saw him Harrison was a privileged twenty-one-year old asshole. Almost as bad as his father, though miles away from his mother's very special brand of asshole.

But it explained how he managed to find Brody. Harrison had all the right connections. The Montgomerys were a four generation political family out of Georgia. The Kennedys without the president, the assassinations, or the sex scandals.

If Harrison wanted to find someone he had enough money and power to see it done.

Interesting, Brody thought. *But why me?*

"What can I do for you, Harrison?"

Harrison sighed and braced his hands on his hips. "We . . . need a man of your talents."

"I'm not all that special." Brody was not in any hurry to get tangled with the Montgomerys again.

"Ashley's been kidnapped."

All of his internal organs recoiled at the mention of her name, and then again at the thought of her in danger.

"Or taken hostage, I'm not . . . I'm not sure what the proper term is."

"Who has her?"

"Somali pirates. She'd been working at a refugee camp in Kenya, had gotten sick, and a friend convinced her to take a vacation in Seychelles. They hired a boat for the day, and I don't know if they got off course, or if the guys on the boat were connected to the pirates—"

"They've held her for ransom?"

"Yes." Harrison shook his head as if he realized he'd been rambling and he was grateful to be shoved back on track.

"We've been negotiating . . ."

Of course the Montgomerys would negotiate.

"How long?"

"Three weeks."

As a rule the Somali pirates didn't hurt their hostages—it was bad for business. But three weeks was a very very long time to be scared.

The thought of Ashley held at gunpoint and mistreated rearranged him. Reduced him to some instinctual, animal level. It wasn't right and he needed to do something about it.

It had been ten years, but in his mind she was seventeen—a protected child, stepping into womanhood. Precocious and ludicrously optimistic. Her presence in a Somali village, surrounded by armed pirates, made about as much sense as that of a unicorn.

"We'll pay, of course. Whatever your fee—"

"What do you need?"

Harrison blinked at Brody's implied agreement, but then Brody had to give the man credit—he sharpened. Focused. Maybe he'd outgrown that genetic asshole problem in his family.

"We've been working with a translator, Umar. Cell phone reception on their end has been a problem but Umar has a satellite phone. And I've got a pilot on the ground outside of Garoowe."

"What do you need?" he repeated.

"We need someone to go get her at the drop-off coordinates. I'd go, but we've been advised that things could get ugly. And we need to keep this . . . quiet."

Of course they did. Harrison's father was up for re-election as Governor of Georgia and, if the rumors were true, Harrison was going to make a shoe-in run for the House of Representatives.

Whatever emotional reaction thoughts of Ashley created in Brody, he managed to bury under logistics.

"What's the timeline?"

"We're supposed to get the coordinates in twelve hours. But they . . . the pirates haven't exactly been reliable."

"How has the ransom been exchanged?" He didn't want to carry around a briefcase of money through the tribal lands of war-torn Somalia.

"We'll transfer it to an offshore account when we get the coordinates and proof that Ashley is alive and safe."

Electronic banking. Offshore accounts. The pirates have come a long way.

"How much?"

"One-point-two million."

Brody laughed, though none of this was funny. "You negotiated down from one and a half?"

Harrison stiffened, reading insult where there was plenty. "Brody, we need you, but you have no idea what this process has been like."

Brody's esteem for the man went up another notch.

He checked his watch. It was two a.m. Brody and the team were flying out of here with the senator at 8 a.m. "You have a plane standing by?"

"The family jet. I can get you as far as Mogadishu, my pilot will pick you up there and fly you to Garoowe, where they've been keeping her. Umar will meet you and take you to Ashley."

"I'll need the satellite number Umar is using."

Harrison, again proving his mettle, handed him a phone. "It's programmed with the numbers of all the people we've been in contact with. As well as a timeline, as complete as we could make it with the little bit of information we have."

Brody took the phone and slipped it in his pocket. He had to finish the Rawlings job, as repugnant as it seemed.

"Have you talked to her?" he asked.

"Once, briefly. They'd been sending photographs, but a week ago I said unless I could actually speak to her—"

"You negotiated."

"Should I have let them shoot her?"

No, he thought, *you should have come and got me three weeks ago.*

"She said she hasn't been hurt," Harrison said. "That she was well fed. Bored, mostly. Scared."

Again, the thing with his lungs.

"We can leave in six hours," Brody said.

Harrison sighed like he'd been holding his breath for days. "Thank you."

Accepting Montgomery gratitude was heavily ironic and oddly difficult, like swallowing a golf ball. But he managed a nod.

"You can wait here in the guesthouse. Try to get some sleep."

"We haven't discussed any payment."

"We will."

Brody was about to knock on the front door to fill Clint in on some of the changes he was going to need to make to the itinerary. But he stopped at the edge of shadow and looked over his shoulder at the golden Montgomery child. A thirty-one year old man now. It had been ten years.

Ashley would be a woman.

He pushed the thought, errant and useless, away. "Why me?"

Harrison's eyes were older and they told a story about the last ten years, and it wasn't a happy one. "We know you'll keep it quiet."

Brody nearly laughed. Yes, he'd proven he could keep the Montgomerys' secrets.

He pushed open the door, but Harrison's voice stopped him. "Brody. Get her and get her home and . . . keep her safe."

So much easier said than done with Ashley Montgomery.